T0156912

The Rescueteers' Christmas Mission

Book 2

Annette O'Leary-Coggins

iUniverse, Inc.
New York   Bloomington

The Rescueteers' Christmas Mission
Book 2

iUniverse books may be ordered through booksellers or by contacting:

iUniverse
1663 Liberty Drive
Bloomington, IN 47403
www.iuniverse.com
1-800-Authors (1-800-288-4677)

Because of the dynamic nature of the Internet, any Web addresses or links contained in this book may have changed since publication and may no longer be valid. The views expressed in this work are solely those of the author and do not necessarily reflect the views of the publisher, and the publisher hereby disclaims any responsibility for them.

ISBN: 978-1-4502-3087-2 (sc)
ISBN: 978-1-4502-3085-8 (dj)
ISBN: 978-1-4502-3086-5 (ebk)

Library of Congress Control Number: 2010907687

Printed in the United States of America

iUniverse rev. date: 7/27/2010

CHAPTER ONE

In the early morning just three days before Christmas, when the air outside makes even the fireplace snap with cold, nine year old Nanny tossed and turned in a frenzy, then awoke as she kicked hard at her blankets.

She repeated several times, "let's get out of here, Henry Daly, let's get out of here." She quickly sat up clutching her blankets to her chest.

Henry Daly, Nanny's beloved brindle greyhound scrambled to his feet ready to protect his best friend with his typical courage. He jumped from Nanny's bed with a yelp and ran to her bedroom's closed door. He let out a series of loud quick barks as he turned his head in all directions looking for a predator.

Nanny's bedroom door burst open. Two figures were silhouetted in the light in the hallway.

"Grr," growled Henry Daly as he took a single step toward them.

"Nanny," said a concerned familiar voice, "are you all right?" Nanny's mom came bustling in, followed by her dad, who flipped on the light. Nanny glanced around her room in a daze. She suddenly recognized her surroundings and realized she must have been having a nightmare. "I just had a bad dream," she said.

Nanny patted her bed, indicating to Henry Daly to jump back up beside her. Henry gladly obliged. "I'm fine now," said Nanny reassuringly.

"What was your dream about, Nanny?" Mom showed her concern by scooching Nanny over and sitting on the edge of the bed. "Do you feel feverish?" To find this out herself, Mom reached over and put her hand on Nanny's forehead.

"I can't remember," answered Nanny with a forced smile.

Her mom tsked and said, "Well, no fever, thank goodness."

Nanny lay back down while Henry Daly turned a few times in a circle and plopped next to Nanny's feet.

"I'm okay now, Mom and Dad," she assured her parents, hoping they couldn't tell that she was really scared. She didn't want to tell them what her nightmare was about, the frightening events that really had happened to her just the summer before.

During her last summer vacation Nanny, her new friend Ned Franey, and Henry Daly found themselves on a rescue mission with King Brian, king of the leprechauns of Coolrainy, in the Banshee's Cradle in the heart of the forest. Nanny kept dreaming about being inside the Cradle again, being hunted down by the Banshee and her skeleguards. Nanny knew she couldn't tell her parents about what she dreamed. Either they'd think she was making it all up for attention, or they might somehow find out the truth about being in the Banshee's Cradle without their permission. She didn't know which was worse, but she did know that no matter what, she'd be grounded for life.

"You'll be getting up in another hour, Nanny," said her mom as she tucked her in. "Why don't you think about what you're asking Santa for this Christmas? It's only three more days now." "Santa should have your letter by now since you mailed it off a week ago."

Nanny's parents nodded to one another obviously feeling like all was well and left the room. But all was not well.

Nanny sat up as if her bed was suddenly lumpy and uncomfortable. Henry Daly quickly stood on all fours and braced himself for another act of courage.

"Henry Daly," she said in a loud whisper, "I had a really bad dream about the Banshee's Cradle. I dreamt we were back in there and Ned and I couldn't find a way out. The Banshee heard you could talk and she wanted a talking greyhound for herself. You were holding our ponies on the Cradle roof for our escape and King Brian didn't answer his whistle. Since Nanny was almost out of breath, she inhaled and continued, "Bull Cullen captured Princess Tara and King Rory, he kept them in a burlap sack somewhere and we couldn't find them. He was going to give them to the Banshee. Do you remember Henry Daly, we were so scared?" Nanny clutched her blanket to her chin. "Don't leave me Henry Daly, stay close to me all the time. I'm afraid."

Henry Daly slathered a host of comforting licks on Nanny's nose. "Don't worry Nanny, I won't leave you," he assured her in a hoarse whisper. I'll never let the Banshee catch us. Grr."

"My goodness, Henry Daly," exhaled Nanny, already feeling the comfort from her beloved greyhound. "I'm so glad I was only dreaming. I already know we're never going back into the Banshee's Cradle ever again." Nanny gave a quick nod. Her untidy auburn curls bounced. "And that's for sure," she said with conviction and a smack on the bed.

CHAPTER TWO

On the day before Christmas Eve, Nanny Reilly and her friend Ned Franey were happy to be finally done with school for the year. They were wrapped up in their winter coats and cowboy hats while fishing at Magandy's Pond. A tall leafless oak tree cast its thick trunk shadow over the dark blue pond making the silver-bellied fish easy to see. Nanny and Ned spotted several good size fish and cast their lines as close to them as they could.

Henry Daly picked up a scent while stalking through the reeds around the pond. "Sniff, sniff, sniff," he meandered through the reeds snuffling at every breath. Something is stirring out there," he said. He raised his head and looked toward the distant forest while sniffing the air, "But it's too far away for me to wander." He looked over his shoulder at Nanny and Ned happily fishing. He remembered his promise to Nanny that he was going to stay close to her all the time. He then turned toward the oak trees and underlying ferns again. "Something is stirring out there. I don't know what it is but it doesn't feel good. I must stay alert."

"No more homework for two weeks," said Ned. Ned's scholastic skills were quite impressive. All the answers came to him very quickly, he wrote them down in a hurry because he was always eager to tuck his pony Bertie in for the night. He and Nanny had a regime. Every evening after his homework, he would meet Nanny at the village stables and groom his pony, while Nanny catered to her flashy white pony, Frosty.

"No more getting up early," said Nanny, who was sick of getting up at 6:30, when it was still pretty dark to get the 'night knots' as her mother called them, out of her thick auburn curls. Every morning Nanny faced a grueling ritual of her mother tussling with her tangles. Nanny constantly squirmed and whined. She always made it out to be worse than it was, as her mother was always careful not to hurt Nanny. In fact, Mrs. Reilly really wanted Nanny to brush her own hair, but Nanny did such a pitiful job it was ten times the work the next morning. "Every morning before school my mom brushes the night knots out of my hair and it takes forever."

Ned threw his eyes up to heaven and shook his head. "That's nothing, you're lucky you don't have to take out the trash like I do, it's heavy and it smells," answered Ned. "That's ten times worse than having your hair brushed."

Nanny frowned at Ned's answer—she was expecting a little sympathy. "It also hurts," she added in the hopes that Ned would see things her way.

"Then you should brush your hair yourself," said Ned, "because you're not going to hurt yourself."

This conversation didn't appeal to Nanny at all. "You sound like my mom," snipped Nanny as she sneeringly quoted her mom's words to her that very morning. "It's time you put a solid effort into brushing your own hair Nanny, you're almost ten years old now. What would Santa think of you if he saw you now?" Nanny thought about what she just said. Forget about sympathy from Ned, what would Santa think of her if he saw her whine like a big baby?

"Do you think Santa knows everything about us?" Nanny asked Ned as she reeled in her line to replace the bait that was stolen by a clever trout. She certainly didn't want Santa to know she whined every morning. How would he know? Would that affect the contents of her letter to him?

"I hope not," answered Ned.

"I hope not too," agreed Nanny, "but what if he does know everything about us?"

"Then maybe he's going to tear up our letters when he gets them," giggled Ned.

"My mom said he should have my letter by now, I mailed it a week ago," said a Nanny, whose worrying made it hard for her to bait her hook.

Henry Daly was still standing with both eyes on the distant forest but he had both ears on Nanny and Ned. He heard Nanny's worried tone of voice, and watched as she counted out the days of the week on her fingers.

"Today is Sunday." She raised her thumb and extended each finger as she counted. "Yesterday was Saturday, the day before that was Friday," Nanny went through seven fingers all the way back to Monday. "Do you think my letter would make it from Coolrainy to the North Pole in seven days?" she asked Ned. "What if it got caught in the mail and doesn't make it in time?"

To get Nanny's mind off her concerns, Ned changed the subject. "I'm mad at myself for taunting all the village children, even you Nanny. Why did you become my friend when I was so mean to you?"

"Because King Brian granted me three wishes," Nanny said, moving her pole around so she could try to find a better spot to attract the fish. "My second wish was that you would stop being mean to me and everyone else. You had to know we were fed up with you, every time we saw you come toward us we went the other way."

Ned frowned. "I'm sorry Nanny," he said. He pretended to punch her arm and said, "Isn't it great that King Brian granted your wish? now you have the coolest friend ever—me." He reeled in his line.

Nanny continued, "Anyway, you don't have to worry like I do Ned, because I wished your meaness away from you six months ago. I was whining about my hair just this morning."

Henry Daly left his post and trotted over to Nanny, a doggy grin across his snout. "You don't have to worry either, Nanny," he said to her in his scratchy voice. "Santa will forgive you for whining, he does every year."

"You're right, Henry Daly," said Nanny. "I've been whining for years and it hasn't ever affected my Christmas gift from Santa."

"Tell me what you asked Santa for, then I'll tell you what I asked him for." Ned was tickled with himself with his Christmas gift request from Santa. "I bet you're going to want the same as me."

"I asked him for a cowgirl suit with fringes like Annie Oakley's." Nanny giggled. "You didn't ask for a cowboy suit, did you, Ned? Last Christmas I got my hat." Nanny patted her tan hat on her head. "With the whole outfit, I'll be a real cowgirl. I'll have my hat, my pony Frosty, and my cowgirl clothes." She cast her freshly baited line out as if she was lassoing the trout.

"You won't have cowboy boots and spurs," said Ned, that's what I asked for. And a red bandana like the Lone Ranger's." Ned carried his fishing pole and stalked the bank following a nice sized trout.

Nanny sighed and tugged on her fishing pole. "I have my sneakers," she quickly replied, "but I wish I'd asked for boots and spurs. Do you think it's too late to send Santa another letter?"

Ned barked a laugh and stopped stalking his fish. You can't send a letter to Santa this late. You're going to have to wait until next year."

Nanny frowned, Ned was right. "Why didn't I think of boots and spurs," she said.

"You know Annie Oakley has dusty boots and spurs like the Lone Ranger's," said Ned, "and every time she takes a step on a wooden floor you can hear her heavy boots and spurs hit the ground. The sound of her metal spurs and slow heavy steps scares everybody and they don't want to mess with her." Ned placed his fishing pole on the grass and demonstrated how Annie Oakley walked. He jagged his thumbs in the front pockets of his jeans and walked slowly with a deliberate swagger away from Nanny.

"See?" Ned said. "If I was walking on a wooden floor instead of grass you would hear, thud clank, thud clank and you wouldn't mess with me because I'd sound really tough."

Ned was right, thought Nanny. "Why didn't you tell me last week before I sent my letter to Santa that you were asking for boots and spurs?" She let out a little more line.

"I didn't think of it until now that you were going to want what I want," said Ned, he picked up his fishing pole and continued stalking the bank. "Anyway, you have your sneakers."

Nanny scowled. "Well, at least I asked for my cowgirl suit."

For a few moments, Henry Daly listened to Nanny's woes and Ned's logic. Then his attention was brought to a visitor standing only three yards behind Nanny. Henry acknowledged the visitor with a broad smile across his snout and a wag of his tail.

"What do you think King Brian is asking Santa for?" asked Nanny

"I bet he's asking Santa for a cowboy hat like ours. He's always saying how fine looking our hats are," answered Ned as he straightened the dark brown cowboy hat on his head.

"Yeah," replied Nanny. "I bet you're right. You certainly are good at picking Christmas gifts. You're right about the boots and spurs. I bet you're right about King Brian's wish too." Nanny nodded her head, making her curls bounce underneath her hat.

"I'm going to blow on my gold whistle and ask King Brian what he wants for Christmas?" She dug deep into her jeans pockets searching for her gold whistle. She had quite a few miscellaneous items in her pockets.

"I love my chainyalleys," said Nanny. She held three multicolored marbles in her hand. "I wonder if Tommy Riordan is still upset with me for beating him at marbles and winning his three best chainyalleys."

"You won those fair and square, Nanny," said Ned. "I had to keep my eye on Tommy Riordan, since he was trying to gain extra inches and cheat you out of your winnings. He knew you were going to beat him and he wasn't liking it one bit been beat by a girl."

"Lucky for me I won," said Nanny. "They're the best marbles I've ever had." Nanny put her coveted chaineyally's back in her pocket and retrieved a small black velvet pouch. Inside the pouch was a gold whistle given to Nanny by King Brian to call on him when she needed him.

"Maybe I should blow on this whistle every morning before and ask King Brian to help me with my hair," said Nanny.

"That's cheating," responded Ned. "You're only supposed to blow on the whistle when you're in distress or when you want to find out how he is."

Nanny and Ned were so busy talking for a moment, they didn't hear a voice call out to them. Within moments, they heard from a familiar voice, "Saints preserve us." The voice cackled, "The two of you have more subjects to talk about than my leprechaun's encyclopedia. Your talking takes you off into a world of your own. Could you not hear me talking to the pair of you? I told you there was no need to blow the whistle--I'm already here. But on and on went the two of you without stopping for a breath. Chainyalley's, boots and spurs, curly hair."

It was King Brian. He stood a proud ten inches tall on top of a spotted mushroom, his fine regalia making him look taller and quite regal. His gold crown was laced with emerald rubies and glistened in the winter sun. His green cloak with gold trim complimented his green and gold checkered waistcoat.

"King Brian," yelled Nanny as she turned in his direction. Without noticing the fish nibble on her bait, she quickly threw her pole down on the grass bank and gave King Brian a big smile. "We were just talking about you."

Ned carried his pole with him to King Brian's side. "Nanny wants to know what you're asking Santa for this Christmas. I bet you're asking for fine cowboy hats like ours."

Then suddenly King Brian's body deflated as he lowered his head. What he was about to tell Nanny Reilly, Ned Franey, and Henry Daly was going to shatter their Christmas wishes and the wishes of every child all over Ireland and around the world. What on earth could be a harder thing to tell them? He took a deep breath and said, "I'm afraid I have some very disappointing news for the three of you. Santa won't be making his way down your chimney tomorrow night."

In the back of Nanny's mind was her habitual whining every morning. "So Santa does know everything about us," she said. "I knew it--he knows about my hair."

"I don't bully anyone anymore. Do I Nanny?" said Ned. He turned to Nanny to vouch for his exceptional behavior. "I changed my ways and now I'm as good as I can be, especially all this week."

Nanny nodded at King Brian while Henry Daly danced at the leprechaun's feet. Ned's right, he has stopped bullying everybody since last summer and now we all like him," she said.

"And I haven't chased a rabbit for three days now," added Henry Daly. Henry looked around and sniffed the air to see if there were any rabbits in the immediate area to show King Brian how well behaved he was.

"Rest assured," answered King Brian, "it's not anything any of you have done or not done." With his hands on his thighs he squatted and sat on the mushroom. His face tightened. He removed his crown with his left hand and ran his right hand over his brow, down the back of his head and rested it on the back of his neck while cradling the glorious crown on his lap.

"What is it, King Brian?" asked Nanny with concern. The little king had doom and gloom written all over him.

King Brian placed his crown back on his head and snapped his fingers. Two mushrooms appeared behind Nanny and Ned, but bigger and far sturdier.

"Have a seat," he said softly, waving his hand toward the brown, cushiony toadstools. Nanny and Ned sat carefully while Henry Daly plopped on the ground at Nanny's feet. Nanny worried: what could King Brian possibly need to tell them that was making him so sad?

"Our old enemy, the Banshee has kidnapped Santa Claus," sighed King Brian. Nanny, Ned, and Henry Daly instantly jumped to their feet.

"But that can't be," exclaimed Nanny. "Nobody kidnaps Santa." She sputtered, "He's—he's, well, he's just Santa. We <u>need</u> him."

"What about Christmas?" said Ned. "We can't have Christmas without Santa."

"I knew something was stirring," said Henry Daly in his scratchy voice. "I could smell it in the air and it's coming from Raven's Point." Henry Daly put his nose in the air to prove his superior smelling capabilities. He growled, "We'll have to go get Santa."

"Can't we just wave our magic shillelaghs you gave us and get him back?" suggested Nanny.

"Yeah," said Ned, thankful for an instant solution to the problem. Even though the former bully didn't say so, the mere thought of the Banshee and her dark dismal world gripped his whole body with fear. Since last summer, he had made a secret vow to himself after his last encounter with the Banshee and her skeleguards, he would never return to the Banshee's Cradle ever again, no matter what.

"If only it was that simple," replied King Brian. "Since our last visit to the Banshee's Cradle, that awful creature has created a fortress of no return. My best leprechaun scout reports that the walls surrounding the Cradle have a wish-blocking device installed. This means," the king said, lowering his voice, "that all wishes and shillelagh waving in the Cradle are null and void. Not only that," he whispered, "the security is tenfold and the Banshee has offered a mighty reward for the capture of the Rescueteers."

"That's us." Nanny's voice trembled with the rest of her body. "My nightmare is coming true. What are we going to do? We aren't really going back into the Banshee's Cradle, are we?"

"If the Banshee gets a hold of us she'll have our hides," added Ned. His voice also trembled as an instant rush of goose bumps invaded his entire body and froze him on the spot. "Are we the only ones in Ireland that can save him? Surely there must be somebody else. Anybody?"

"There is someone else," said King Brian, his voice strengthening. "We're going to call in the troops." He jumped from his mushroom stool landing both feet squarely on the ground and abruptly stood to attention. Nanny began to feel a little relieved that he appeared to have control over the whole situation, and knew exactly what to do.

"Never let it be said that the Banshee outwitted King Brian, king of all the leprechauns of Coolrainy. I'm too long in the tooth for the likes of that to happen." The king's body language read cock of the walk again. He stood tall and proud with his typical regal stance.

Nanny, Ned, and Henry Daly immediately stood to attention, they put their right hand at their foreheads and saluted. Henry Daly stuck his tail straight up.

"Does that mean we don't have to go?" asked Nanny. "That would be nice."

"I'd love to tell you that we don't have to go, Nanny Reilly," answered King Brian."I know the Banshee's Cradle is a very scary place, but unfortunately we have to go. We're the Rescueteers, there's nobody else who can go in our place. This time is going to be a whole lot worse than the last time, and we badly need extra help." King Brian smiled with assurance. "But not to worry, I know exactly who to call."

Nanny and Ned didn't feel as brave as King Brian did, even though they were the Rescueteers. Henry Daly faced the forest and gave several quick sniffs at the air. "I knew I could smell trouble," he said, "big trouble."

"I hope you call on somebody big and strong like Bull Cullen," said Ned.

"Someone a whole lot bigger than the Banshee to scare the living daylights out of her."

If Santa was going to be rescued and Christmas was going to be saved, the Rescueteers knew they were everybody's only hope. After all, there were the two bravest children in Ireland and Henry Daly the bravest dog, or so they had been told.

CHAPTER THREE

"Rescueteers," said King Brian, looking directly into their eyes again. "We have a mission of tremendous importance and great danger before us. The Christmas joy of every child in the world rests on our shoulders."

King Brian reached into his coat pocket. He dug deep and pulled out a black velvet pouch exactly like the one Nanny had retrieved her gold whistle from moments earlier. He unraveled the gold braided cord around the pouch and retrieved his very own gold whistle. He held the whistle before him and said, "This is the first time ever in my long lifetime that I have resorted to blowing on my own whistle for help. I never thought the day would come." His bearded jaws ballooned as he blew hard on the gold whistle.

A sudden wind arose. The reeds around Magandy's Pond began to rustle and shimmer. Three white twelve-inch tall tornados glided across the pond and stopped at the Rescueteers.

"Don't let them get me, Henry Daly," whispered Nanny as she and Ned took a step back. Henry Daly stood in front of Nanny and Ned. He growled fiercely, showing his saliva drooling fangs; the hackles on his neck were rigid. The tornados continued to spin.

"The troops have arrived," smiled King Brian rubbing his hands together. "Stand back now lads, and lassie," he glanced at Nanny with a smile, "and give them some room."

Nanny and Ned took three more steps back. Ned caught Nanny's hand. Henry Daly growled again, this time his hackles were down, but his fangs still showed. He stepped back and allowed the spinning tornados to stop. The wind died down and all was quiet around Magandy's Pond.

"What kind of troops are they?" asked Ned. "They look like spinning big tops to me."

"How are spinning tops going to help us in the Banshee's Cradle?" asked Nanny.

"Nanny Reilly, Ned Franey and Henry Daly," said King Brian, "meet the troops."

Nanny and Ned kept quiet. Henry Daly stopped growling. The three tornados now appeared to be white spinning top-shaped tents with zippers from top to bottom. One of the zippers was pulled down and pair of small hands opened the zipper door. King Rory, King Brian's brother stuck his head out, he looked left and right and up and down.

"It's only me, King of the leprechauns of Ballineskar greeting you with my royal presence. Don't be alarmed." His round red-bearded face wore a broad smile. His polished red rosy cheeks brought attention to his jolly face. His emerald studded gold crown was tilted on his head after his splendid spinning top entrance. He stepped out of his tent and straightened his crown. He wore a solid green waistcoat and a green checkered cloak with gold trim. He kicked his heels together and danced the first dozen steps of an Irish jig. He finished with a stamp of his right foot on the ground, leaned toward his captive audience wrapping his cloak around his torso and bowed with a smile.

"Nanny Reilly, Ned Franey and Henry Daly," he said in his leprechaun brogue. "Sure isn't the pleasure is all mine." King Rory looked up at Nanny and Ned. Saints preserve us, sure haven't you all shot up like mushrooms since I saw you last."

Ned straightened himself up to appear even taller. "I'm six inches taller than Nanny now," he smiled and looked down at Nanny. "Nanny is only nine, I'm ten"

"You just turned ten a week ago," said Nanny. "I'm going to be ten in three and a half more weeks." Nanny held up three fingers showing what she thought was a very short amount of time.

Before anyone could respond, the second zipper was undone, a familiar face peered through and looked left and right and all around. The little man was admiring his surroundings. "What a grand little meadow with Magandy's Pond nestled in the middle, sure aren't we very fortunate." The face greeted Nanny, Ned, and Henry Daly with a smile.

"King Brian," said Nanny, "what are you doing in there, when you're also out here?"

"I've learned a trick or two in my day, and one of them happens to be," he paused for a moment and said, "how can I be there, when I'm here? Figure that one out, Nanny Reilly lass," he chuckled. King Rory was chuckling hard in the background at these familiar leprechaun antics, like appearing and disappearing.

"Would you excuse me for one moment please," said the peeping face and quickly pulled his head back into the protective tent. Not another sound was heard from him.

"I bet he's just sitting in there," said Ned as he began to approach the tent to investigate the matter.

"My dear lad," answered King Brian's voice, "how can I be there when I'm here?" Nanny, Ned, and Henry Daly turned their attention from their protective tent to King Brian's toadstool behind them. King Brian was standing straight and tall with his fists on his hips and another grin across his face.

Henry Daly yelped and wagged his tail vigorously. He was enjoying this guessing game.

"How can you do that?" asked Nanny, "can you show me how to do that?

King Rory laughed out with more heavy chuckles. He was enjoying the antics of his brother immensely.

"I think that's going to be a little more difficult than you think," King Brian's voice boomed from the protective tent. "Sure, you have to be born into a special kind of magic like that."

Nanny, Ned, and Henry Daly quickly turned to see King Brian's head once again sticking out of the tent. This time, without further ado he stepped out of the tent and stood tall with his fists on his hips and his trickster smile showing all his teeth.

Henry Daly yelped again, "What fun this is. It's far better than fetch."

"What do you mean by born into it?" asked Ned.

"I mean I'm King Brendan," chuckled the lookalike leprechaun king.

"You look just like King Brian," said Nanny, looking at one and then the other.

"Of course I do," replied the familiar face with that cheeky glint in his eye. "My brother Brian and I are identical twins. I'm King Brendan, king of all the leprechauns of Ballyvaloo." He wore the exact attire and the same dance shoes as his brother King Brian did. He even carried his body the same way, in a short but impressive swagger. He put the forefinger of his left hand to his lips and said, "Shh, don't tell anyone, it's the secret to our success," then he winked.

"We didn't know you had a twin brother, King Brian," said Nanny as she continued to look back and forth as if the two brothers were standing on opposites sides of a mirror.

"Why weren't you at the dance with us on midsummer's eve?" asked Ned. "How come we only met King Rory?"

"Because lad, as I said before, it's the best kept secret to our success in the world of leprechauns. Every leprechaun king has a twin. It's one of our royal perks. King Brendan chuckled accompanied by King Brian and King Rory. "It's best if only one of us shows up at an occasion, otherwise everybody would know, and sure the fun would be gone out of it."

The third tent zipper was unzipped and another red, round familiar face appeared topped by a crown tilted to one side. He stepped out of his tent, danced the first dozen steps of an Irish jig and finished with a stamp of his left foot on the ground. Just like King Rory, he leaned toward Nanny, Ned, and Henry Daly, wrapped his cloak around his torso and bowed with a smile.

"You're King Rory's twin," exclaimed Nanny.

"Yeah," said Ned. "You look just like him."

"I am indeed," was the reply. "My name is King Cormac, king of all the leprechauns of Ballyconniger." He too put his left forefinger to his lips and with the broadest smile said, "Shh, it's also the secret to our long-lived success."

King Brian enjoyed watching Nanny, Ned, and Henry Daly's reaction to the look-alikes. "It's grand to see the pair of you confused and bewildered," he said, "It was an old family secret that had never been shared with anyone outside the leprechaun world before." King Brian bowed and apologized. "Please accept my humble apologies

Nanny Reilly, Ned Franey and Henry Daly. It's just something we don't broadcast. As my brothers told you, longevity runs in the family for that reason." And how right his two brothers were, it really was the secret to their long-lived success.

Henry took a step toward the first tent. He could hear scuffling going on inside. "Grr," he growled, "who's in there?"

Nanny screamed and hid behind Ned. "Get her, Henry Daly, get her," said Nanny. "It's the Banshee looking for the Rescueteers."

"Good boy, Henry Daly," added Ned. "Don't let her get us." Fear gripped Nanny and Ned.

"The Banshee is on the prowl looking for us," said Nanny. "She could come out of anywhere. Ned backed up a step. Nanny, with both her hands clasped tightly to Ned's right arm, backed up a step with him.

The four leprechaun kings stopped laughing. "What could it be, Brother Rory?" asked King Brian. "It's in your protective tent."

"I have no idea," answered King Rory. "I was the only one in there." King Rory walked toward his tent. "Let's find out," he said.

Something was punching at the wall of the tent and grunting.

"Can't a girl have some privacy while she's getting dressed?" announced a distressed voice from inside the tent.

"I know that voice," said Nanny, "that's Princess Tara."

Princess Tara stumbled from the tent making valiant attempts to put her small black right paddock boot on. Her long red untidy hair, (messy because of her journey as she wasn't strapped in like King Rory) covered her whole face. With a big puff, she blew her locks up and out of her eyes. She finally got her boot on, and then used both hands to straighten out her hair. She snapped her fingers and a green velvet bow appeared in her hand to tie up her hair. She wore a dark green riding jacket with gold buttons, a white stock around her neck fixed with a gold pin, and a pair of beige jodhpurs.

"Tara," said King Rory, who twitched as he always did when he was upset. "What are you doing here?" He looked down at her six and a half inch tall frame.

"I saw you leave the burrow in a hurry and you ordered your army to be on standby with all their artillery and your horse. So I sneaked into the protective tent with my riding attire. I wanted to be dressed for action." She raised her small fists up as if she was in a boxing match. "I knew something serious was cooking, so here I am to help." She placed both hands on her hips and smiled a big grin.

"Princess Tara," said Nanny, "it's so good to see you. You're still the same as when I first met you," remembered Nanny. "A feisty little princess with a big punch."

"Hello again, Nanny Reilly," replied the princess. "I suspected yourself, Ned and Henry Daly were part of this whistle-blowing thing."

"It was me who blew the whistle, my sweet little niece," replied King Brian as the smile of enjoyment left his face. "I know only leprechaun royalty use their gold whistles for extreme emergencies, and so far in our lifetime there has never been an extreme emergency," he paused for a breath, "until this very day." The other three kings and Princess Tara looked at King Brian with solemn faces wondering why, after an entire lifetime, what the extreme emergency could possibly be?

Nanny, Ned, and Henry Daly lowered their heads. They knew the answer.

"You look like it's the end of the world, Brother Brian," said King Cormac. "It can't be that bad, can it?" He looked deep into his brother's eyes and realized that yes, it was that bad.

"In a sense, it's the end of the world, Brother Cormac, at least the end of the Christmas world as we know it. My beloved family," sighed King Brian, "I sadly regret to report to you that the Banshee has defied belief and kidnapped Santa Claus."

"No," exclaimed Princess Tara, "she wouldn't dare. Why would she want to kidnap him? Tomorrow is Christmas Eve. She's despicable. If I see her I'll punch her on the nose as hard as I can." Princess Tara struck out with her right fist clenched demonstrating her powerful punch.

"Tara," said King Rory, surprised by his tiny daughter's sudden burst of anger. He had a more refined image of her.

"Me too," added Ned as he raised both fists in front of his face like a boxer. "I know how to throw a left hook and knock her out." These were brave words from Ned, but unbeknownst to his audience, Ned was terrified and his mind was already made up about his return to the Banshee's Cradle.

'You're very brave Ned, and you too Princess Tara," said Nanny. "I don't think I want to see the Banshee, let alone punch her in the nose and give her a left hook." Nanny was silently hoping to find her brave heart before she stepped foot inside the Cradle again.

"Do you have any ideas, Brian?" asked King Brendan, knowing that his brother was the craftiest leprechaun who walked the planet and always had a way out of a sticky situation. "How can we help?"

"We need to put our heads together and come up with an invincible plan," replied King Brian. He explained to the kings what his top leprechaun scout had reported back to him. "There's a wish-blocking device, and she has her skeleguards doubled and on high alert. We're only going to get one chance at this, and we need to act fast. We have 24 hours to get Santa back on his sleigh with his reindeers.

Nanny, Ned, and Henry Daly looked at each other knowing what King Brian meant. On that summer night in the Cradle on their previous rescue mission to save Fran O'Toole and Mike Donovan, They had already witnessed the victims of the Banshee being carted off to departures never to return. Getting Santa back was a mass rescue mission they were about to venture on. More than Santa's freedom was at stake.

"Does this mean we're for sure going back inside the Banshee's Cradle?" asked Ned.

"We have to, lad," answered King Brian, "As sworn in Rescueteers for the good of mankind and animal kind, it's our duty, we have no choice.

King Rory, King Cormac, King Brendan, and Princess Tara too understood how deeply earnest King Brian's grave words were. A solemn silence surrounded Magandy's Pond.

CHAPTER FOUR

"I'm finding all this hard to believe," said Nanny. "Twenty minutes ago we were fishing and my only concerns were boots, spurs, and my hair. Now I don't care about all that. I have other things a whole lot worse on my mind."

Henry Daly showed his concern for Nanny's new woe as he sat and placed his paw on her leg "I won't let the Banshee get us," he assured her.

"Isn't that the truth Nanny Reilly, in an instant everything can change," said King Cormac. "I was just about to enjoy a big bowl of Irish stew with homemade bread straight from the oven—I was really looking forward to it. I had my lunch table all set and I was salivating. Now I couldn't eat a thing, my stomach is queasy thinking about poor Santa and the dilemma he's in."

"Are we going now?" asked Ned. "I don't think I'm ready to go this minute."

"We should all go home first," said King Brian, "and get some food into our stomachs, and plenty of rest. It's to our advantage to go on this mission when it's dark and we can't be seen so easily. We'll meet back here at Magandy's Pond at midnight and leave then. You're going to need your ponies," he continued, "so feed them plenty of oats before we take off on this mission. They, like the rest of us, are going to need every ounce of energy they have in them."

"But we've no time to go home, King Brian," replied Nanny. "What about Santa? We'll have to leave now."

"Nanny is right, Uncle Brian," said Princess Tara. "Let's go now." Princess Tara pulled on her hair from behind and tightened her ponytail.

"We can just snap our fingers and have Bertie and Frosty here in the blink if an eye," said Nanny. "Besides, going home first would give me too much time to dwell on the whole situation and I might not want to ever venture outdoors again. I'll be wondering if the Banshee is lurking in the shadows looking for me."

Ned was having terrifying thoughts. In fact, he wanted to go straight home that very second and lock his bedroom door behind him. "I think we should go home first like King Brian said, Nanny. We need more time."

"Let's go now, all five of you can ride on my back," suggested Henry Daly as he walked toward the leprechaun contingent. He bowed before them, giving them permission to climb aboard. He was ready to go straight away. He didn't have an ounce of fear.

Henry knew the little people didn't weigh much and with his magical abilities he could fly them off into the heavens very easily.

"Now hold your horses, you young lads and lassies," said King Brian holding his right hand high in the air. "Sure we can't just get up and go without some sort of a plan."

"Indeed that's very true," added King Rory, nodding. "If we fail to plan our strategies, we'll surely fail on our mission. We need a good plan to get into the Cradle and a better plan to get us all out." King Rory glanced at Princess Tara with a worried frown. He now had a new nine-year-old concern added to the dilemma.

King Cormac and King Brendan both chuckled at the same time as they listened to the impulsive responses from Nanny, Princess Tara and Henry Daly.

"Sometimes 'tis a grand thing to be young and foolish," smiled King Brendan, but not today."

"Sure, we understand your anxiety," said King Cormac. "Santa is a grand man, and none of us want to see him imprisoned by the Banshee at any time of the year, especially the day before Christmas Eve. Don't worry, we'll think of something to get him out. Sure I'm expecting a pair of gold buckles myself," he added.

"You're right, Uncle Brian," said Princess Tara holding her arms out with her palms upright. "When we get to the Banshee's Cradle, what do we do?"

Nanny shuddered at the thought of not being able to snap her fingers or wave her magic shillelagh. "How are we going to save Santa with no magic powers to get us out of trouble?" In an instant, her warm winter coat closed around her, making her feel her body overheat as the sudden realization hit her. Imagine being in the Banshee's Cradle with no magic powers. Terrifying. "You're right Ned, maybe we should go home first and think about this."

"Well now, lass," grinned King Brian, who seemed to have a plan of action already brewing. This was right up King Brian's alley. It seemed like the worse the situation was, the more he embraced it. He placed his thumbs under the lapels of his checkered waistcoat and stood tall and proud. He smiled and looked directly at Henry Daly. "Magic is not always called for when a situation arises. Besides, we have Henry Daly on our side."

Henry pricked his ears and tilted his head to one side. He was wondering what King Brian meant by that. "Yeah, you have me on your side," he assured Nanny in his scratchy voice. "What will I be doing?"

Nanny felt some comfort in Henry's words, but she still felt fear. "Good boy, Henry Daly, I know you won't let anything happen to us, it's just a scary thought going back in the Cradle where that wicked Banshee has no mercy."

Ned stood close to Henry Daly, he too wanted to feed off that assurance. He badly needed some kind of comforting thought to go through his mind. "I'm going to stay close to you all the time, Henry Daly," said Ned. "I know if I'm close to you the Banshee won't come too close to me."

"Well, I'm not one bit afraid of that silly old Banshee," said Princess Tara. "She doesn't scare me.

Ned looked at Princess Tara as she walked confidently toward King Brian. How could a little thing like Princess Tara not be scared he thought? She can't be more than eight inches tall. "You're not afraid because you haven't come face-to-face with her like Nanny and I have. If you saw her mean face and warty nose you be running in the other direction." Then he realized, Princess Tara was not in the Banshee's

Cradle, nor did she come face to face with the Banshee like he and Nanny did.

"I don't care what she looks like," answered Princess Tara, as he looked up at Ned with her arm stretched and holding up five fingers. "If she had five thousand warts on her face she still wouldn't scare me." Princess Tara walked over to King Brian and caught his hand. "You're the craftiest leprechaun in Ireland, Uncle Brian," she said with a smile. "I'm glad both you and Henry Daly are on our side."

All the leprechauns laughed. King Rory, King Cormac and King Brendan had lived a lot of years with King Brian and his crafty old ways. They laughed the loudest. Nanny managed to smile but Ned remained expressionless.

Nanny really wanted to shake her fear. She, like many other children of her age wanted to be some sort of fearless super hero. Now, out of the blue, she was somewhat of super hero, a Rescueteer, a scared Rescueteer with no magic powers just when she needs them most. Sure there's no super hero without magic powers "Perhaps we should make Magandy's Pond our headquarters," said Nanny, in the hopes that a super hero with a headquarters would have no fear.

"Magandy's Pond, I like the sound of that, Nanny Reilly. It's right at my front door—I won't have to travel far," smiled King Brian.

All the Rescueteers agreed and Magandy's Pond was now named the Official Headquarters of the Rescueteers. All strategic planning and rehearsals would be done there.

"Now that we have established Magandy's Pond of Coolrainy as our headquarters," said King Brian. "I must ask King Rory, King Cormac, my twin brother King Brendan, and my lovely niece Princess Tara to stand to attention and raise your right hands in the air."

"I think you should go home, Tara," said King Rory, as he turned Princess Tara toward him with both hands on her shoulders. The thoughts of anything happening to his little princess was too much of a burden for him to carry.

"Don't worry about me, Father," smiled Princess Tara. "I promise I won't do anything stupid."

That's exactly what concerned King Rory. He retrieved his tiny green handkerchief from his trouser pocket and patted away the beads of nervous sweat on his brow. "I'm proud of your fearlessness Tara, and you definitely inherited your Uncle Brian's smarts, but you're still my little princess," he said. He wanted to add, and you're someone who at times can be quite silly, but he kept those thoughts to himself.

The four new arrivals proudly stood and raised their right hands.

King Brian said, "Do you solemnly swear to help in the rescue of Santa Claus and all others from the Banshee's Cradle for the sake of all the children and animals in the world?" He glanced at Henry Daly and winked." Henry Daly gave one of his bright smiles, showing all his teeth and gums.

"I do," answered the four in unison.

"And do you solemnly swear," continued King Brian, "to keep the safety of all other Rescueteers at the forefront of your mind."

"I do," was the answer once again.

"By the power vested in me, King Brian, king of all the leprechauns of Coolrainy, I now pronounce you all Rescueteers." King Brian raised his shillelagh and gently tapped each new member on each shoulder with it. They were now sworn in and bore the title of Rescueteers.

"This is like the Knights of the Round table with King Arthur," said Nanny excitedly. She was beginning to feel a little braver, though she worried it wouldn't be enough, but at least she was headed in the right direction.

"Except we have shillelagh's instead of swords," replied Ned, knowing that this time a sword would be a lot more help to them than a shillelagh inside the Banshee's Cradle.

"We should have a round table," said Nanny thinking that would make their title more official and she would feel even more heroic.

"Indeed we should," replied King Brian. He was keeping things as lighthearted as he could, as he knew Nanny and Ned quite well. He sensed their anxiety, and he, along with King Rory and Princess Tara, didn't want to see them venture into the Banshee's Cradle. However, he knew it was absolutely necessary. He needed their help to get Santa back—he couldn't do it without them. He also knew by giving them an official headquarters and a round table, perhaps a seed of bravery would be planted. He hoped somehow in the next several hours they would rise above their fear. If not, Santa was doomed and many others with him.

King Brian used his most light-hearted voice as he declared, "King Brendan, why don't you do the honors and provide us with the finest round table there is for the brave Rescueteers?"

"Absolutely, Brother Brian," replied King Brendan. He stood to attention, retrieved his shillelagh from underneath his cloak and in grandiose style, pointed it at a vacant spot at the edge of Magandy's Pond. He made precise circular motions with it and said,

> "May we have a table round,
> Not too tall from the ground.
> May our table accommodate eight,
> And may words of wisdom seal our fate."

King Brendan was tickled to be the provider of the finest extra large, flat-topped, round spotted mushroom table. "Didn't I do well?" he said.

"When it comes to wishing, leprechauns really know how to pour it on," said Nanny. The incredible flat-topped mushroom table that stood before her made her think that the fate of Santa was in good hands with the Rescueteers. She was now beginning to feel a little more comfortable with the challenge ahead of them. "I think Santa is going to be just fine."

"All right then, lads and lassies," smiled King Brian, as he threw his cloak over his shoulder and rubbed his hands together. "Gather 'round our new table and let's get started on our rescue mission."

Nanny and Ned sat on their mushroom stools. Henry Daly sat to attention between them. The four kings and Princess Tara sat on the large spotted toadstool.

Four Leprechaun kings, one leprechaun princess, two of the bravest children in Ireland, and a brindle greyhound put their heads together and came up with their invincible plan to rescue Santa Claus.

CHAPTER FIVE

Meanwhile, back at Dreary Castle in the Banshee's Cradle in the heart of the forest, the Banshee was working on her own plans for the festive season. She scurried down her dark, dismal hallway toward her boudoir. Her long black cloak swept the ground leaving a cloud of dust after her every stride. Every twenty yards, a bat perched on an old bone badly nailed into the corridor wall, held a dripping wax candle with a miserable little flame on it.

"Jingle bells, jingle bells," she laughed in her deep hoarse voice. "There'll be no jingling of bells this Christmas, jingling of bones more like it." The Banshee held Santa's hat in her hand. "Such a ridiculous hat. I finally caught that jolly old buzzard who's been dodging me for centuries." With both hands, she forcefully pushed open the heavy oak door of her boudoir and slammed it hard behind her. The draft from the door blew out the bat candles.

One bat flew from his perch to the master flame which was enclosed in a small glass globe over the Banshee's door. He lit his candle again. "She's in rare form tonight, lads," the bat announced as he flew from candle to candle to relight them with his small flame.

Inside the Banshee's quarters was an eerie sight to behold. Uncaringly decorated with cobwebs, a portrait of the Banshee adorned the wall above her four-poster bed. Each poster on her bed had a skeleton hand on it and the spiky fingers acted as hangers for miscellaneous black banshee attire. The Banshee's closet doors were open and falling off the hinges. Only black clothing hung untidily in her closet. Old black boots lined the closet floor.

The Banshee forced her adjoined hands between her closet attire and spread her dusty black clothes widely apart. On the back wall of her closet was a loose red brick. She toyed with the brick using her long fingernails until it separated itself from the other bricks. Then she gently removed the red brick from its slot and placed it on the top shelf of her closet.

> "There are bricks of silver,
> There are bricks of gold.
> There are bricks that are new,
> There are bricks that are old.
> But the best brick of all,
> Is in my closet in the wall."

She retrieved a bunch of keys and fumbled through them. The Banshee held one particular key close to her long crooked nose and smiled an ugly smile.

"My prize captor," she bragged to herself. "I'm about to become the most prestigious Banshee of all." She walked toward her portrait, admiring it at every stride.

"You clever Banshee you," she said. "You're so sneaky. Santa fell for your miserable lies. Oh, Santa," she said in a weak and timid voice, "I really am sorry for all the heartache I have caused you over the centuries. Can you ever forgive me? I've always wanted to enjoy Christmas just like everybody else. I want to feel part of society again. Can you help me? Ha, ha, ha, ha. What a fool to fall for all that gosh-wash. He only got what he deserved for thinking the Banshee had softened. This Banshee will <u>never</u> soften."

An old heavy oak door with blackened brass bolts led down a dark stairway from the Banshee's boudoir to Santa's place of capture. Santa lay face down on a rickety old bed in a stone-walled cell.

'Ho, Ho, Ho," jeered the Banshee. "You don't appear to be so jolly now. I think I know what it is. I think Santa forgot about you this Christmas, ha ha ha."

Santa rolled over, got up, and stood to attention. He calmly brushed the dust that had accumulated from the Banshee's Cradle from his red, festive clothing.

"Banshee," he said in a warm deep voice, "I have no battle with you. I'm giving you a chance to undo this mess you've put yourself in. If you were as clever as you think you are you would let me go so I can finish my preparations for tomorrow night."

"Ha, ha, ha, ha," laughed the Banshee as she clasped her hands together to express her delight. "Nothing and no one can help you now, Mr. Santa Claus." She paused, leaned toward Santa and grabbed the cell bars with her long bony fingers. Her long black fingernails jabbed at her wrists, her long narrow nose pushed between the cell bars. Her voice changed, sounding like death itself. She said, "Only the stupid would make any attempts at a rescue. I have turned Dreary Castle into a fortress like no other. I have designed and implemented an unbreakable device around my castle walls to keep predators out." She cackled, reminding Santa of a witch.

Santa remained calm, even though several hairy warts on the Banshee's nose were a big distraction to him. His deep warm voice remained the same. "Banshee, our conversation is over. You have been given a chance to reverse this situation, but alas, you refuse to do so." Santa turned his back on the Banshee. "Now if you would excuse me, I need to get some sleep before Christmas Eve. Please, if you'd be so kind, dim the lights on your way out." He knelt down, cuddled down to his face down position, and began to snore.

The Banshee was shocked. Never before had a prisoner ever behaved in such a manner toward her. He must know something she didn't. What could it be? If those Rescueteers are planning a great escape for Santa, she was ready for them. The Banshee mumbled to herself all the way up the dark stairwell and back to her boudoir.

"He's only pretending," the Banshee concluded as he threw her bunch of keys back into her secret hiding place and angrily jammed the red brick back into its slot.

"Dreary Castle is invincible. I know that. I need to double-check my plans and make sure I have everything covered from all angles.

"Nobody," she said, "nobody, would even dare to outsmart me again. I'm ready for the Rescueteers. Two silly children, one simple dog, and a foolish leprechaun will meet their match this time. I have a lot of Christmas surprises waiting for them." Her hearty laugh echoed throughout Dreary Castle and all around the Banshee's Cradle.

Santa awoke and lay thinking in his cell. He was hoping he could intimidate the Banshee into letting him go. He didn't know anything about the Rescueteers. He just knew from his scouting elves on good and bad behavior that that there was two exceptionally good children named Nanny Reilly and Ned Franey, especially Ned, who'd struggled with being mean but had changed into a nice young man. Santa was also aware of an exceptionally good dog named Henry Daly. Old St. Nick had jotted all of their names down in his book for a special Christmas gift. He also knew from his scouting elves, a leprechaun King named King Brian had shown remarkable improvement toward the good of mankind. He too was down in Santa's book for a special gift.

Santa then heard the laughter of the Banshee, and shuddered, then began to cry. Tears rolled down his rosy red cheeks. What about the children around the world, he worried. "Never another Christmas ever? No more Christmas carols? No more Christmas cheer? No more Christmas anything." He felt doomed. Santa pressed his tear-stained face into his hands and sobbed.

CHAPTER SIX

The Rescueteers were huddled closely around their round mushroom table. Heads were continuously nodding acknowledging everyone's role in the rescue of Santa Claus. Each one had a specific task. If one Rescueteer failed, they all failed. Just one mistake, or one strategy out of sequence and they were are all doomed.

"Well now Rescueteers," said King Brian after their meeting. The twinkle in his eye and the broad smile across his narrow red face gave the children confidence. "Sure, the Banshee won't know what hit her. One of the most difficult things to do on this planet is to outsmart a leprechaun."

"But I remember outsmarting you just a very short time ago at this very spot, King Brian," smiled Nanny Reilly. Nanny grinned at Princess Tara, who also remembered outsmarting King Brian with the Darby O'Gill two-step right there at Magandy's Pond.

"It takes a leprechaun to know a leprechaun," was Princess Tara's reply, "and I know Uncle Brian quite well."

King Rory, King Cormac, and King Brendan all laughed heartily, holding their chubby bellies with their hands.

"Sure, Brian didn't know at the time that Nanny Reilly was under the influence of the smartest leprechaun Princess that Ireland has ever known," chuckled Tara's proud dad King Rory.

"Well, my dear Princess Tara," replied a smiling King Brian, "you're about to get another chance at putting your leprechaun smarts to the test. Lads, lassies, and Henry Daly, we all need to rehearse our roles for our guest appearance at the Banshee's Cradle tonight.

The broad smiles left everyone's faces. Nanny Reilly put her arm around her faithful greyhound, who thumped his tail on the green grass. "You, me and Ned are first up, Henry Daly," she said nervously.

"Don't worry, Nanny," he replied. He gently licked Nanny's nose. Then he turned to Ned and licked his hand. Ned took a deep swallow. He wanted to say out loud that he was afraid and not going no matter what. But the words wouldn't come out.

All Ned could think about was how was he going to get out of this predicament he was in? He didn't want to be a Rescueteer anymore.

"King Brian is right," said Henry Daly. "Sure the Banshee won't know what hit her, and Santa will be leaving our gifts under the tree tomorrow night."

Nanny sighed and smiled all in the one breath, as did all the other Rescueteers, except Ned.

"What would I ever do without you by my side, Henry Daly? I'm so glad I wished you could talk just to hear you say what you just said."

Nanny gave Henry Daly a big hug. "Let's do it," she said, and realized she was feeling braver by the minute.

Nanny, Ned, and Henry Daly rehearsed without flaw. King Brendan was next on center stage to play his part. Princess Tara and King Rory were up next to rehearse their roles. The last pair to rehearse for the grand finale was King Brian and King Cormac. They played their roles to perfection. Everybody was foot perfect. However, rehearsals can go well when nobody is under pressure. The success of their mission depended on their state of mind at the time and the Banshee herself. What did she have in store for them? Would she fall into their trap, or would she herself have a trap of her own for the Rescueteers to fall into?

CHAPTER SEVEN

Back in the Banshee's boudoir, the Banshee checked her doors and windows were locked tight. "It doesn't do any harm to double-check things at a time like this," she said. "Even though I already know my plans are invincible." She stomped her foot hard on a loose floorboard and it popped up. She threw the floorboard to one side and retrieved several rolls of rawhide, tied together with braided ponytails. She tossed a bundle of rumpled up blankets to one end of her bed, unrolled the rawhides and spread them out on her bed.

"Mmm, let me see what I have here." The old witch stuck her nose close to the first rawhide and squinted with her beady black eyes. "Main entrance," she mumbled as she ran her long bony forefinger over the rawhide. "Wish-blocking device on. Good. Well, that seems to be set in concrete. I can't see how any silly leprechaun or two stupid children and one dumb dog can infiltrate The Banshee's Cradle."

She rolled up that particular rawhide and reached for the second one. "Dungeons," she said. Again she ran her long bony finger over the rawhide. "Everything seems to be in order there. I'm so clever," she chuckled to herself as she rolled up that rawhide and unraveled the third one.

"Secret Tunnel," she said, repeating the same process with her bony finger as she studied the rawhide. "Ha, ha, ha," she laughed. "How can I be so brilliant? I'm the smartest Banshee I know."

She took a step back and clasped her hands together. "Now is the time for the Banshee to shine. My very own world is about to materialize. I'll soon have all the silly people of Coolrainy, Ballineskar. Ballyvaloo and Ballyconniger in the Banshee's Cradle. Their silly Santa Claus, the fool who gives to them instead of taking from them, will no longer exist. I'll eliminate all that hogwash stuff like giving, and happiness, and Christmas wishes. There's nobody as clever as me, and whoever should dare to outsmart me will end up in departures for sure."

The Banshee rolled up her rawhide scrolls and placed them back in their hiding place. Then she stomped hard on the floorboard beside it and that popped up. "My greatest plan of all," she chuckled to herself. "The development plan for the Banshee's Cradle, encompassing all the surrounding lands occupied by my very own future residents, ha ha ha."

Once again, the Banshee's laughter rang throughout Dreary Castle and all around the Cradle, sending shivers down the spine of Santa Claus who lay in that miserable dungeon praying for a miracle.

CHAPTER EIGHT

This was like déjà vu for Nanny. Here she was again lying in bed in her clothes with Henry Daly by her side. The two friends were about to slip out her bedroom window to rendezvous at Magandy's Pond with the rest of her intrepid comrades. Nanny thought back to that first midnight encounter with King Brian when he tricked her into kidnapping Princess Tara. How boring that seemed now compared to what lay ahead.

"Do you remember when we met King Brian for the first time last summer, Henry Daly?" Henry's tail slowly thumped of the bed post, he remembered with a smile. "We kidnapped Poor Princess Tara and put her in a burlap sack, but that doesn't seem like a big deal anymore," said Nanny.

She lay in her bed listening for the quiet night sounds. "I think everybody has gone to bed, Henry Daly," whispered Nanny. "Let's put our checklist together." Nanny took a deep breath and sighed. "Just thinking of what lies ahead makes me want to throw up, even though I know we have a good plan. But now is not the time to think the worst, now is the time to get ready for the biggest rescue mission we may ever have to go on."

Nanny quietly pulled back the bedclothes and slid out of bed. She was fully dressed and ready for action. She looked down at her sneakers. "Why didn't I think of boots and spurs?" She frowned about her thoughtlessness. Now they were another year away. Nanny put her cowboy hat on and slowly strutted her way across her bedroom. She was imitating Ned imitating Annie Oakley. She imagined the clank of the spurs and the sound of her leather boots on a wooden floor. Then she imagined her fringed Annie Oakley cowgirl suit. She was part of the American Wild West. She felt good and she felt brave. She paused and casually turned to Henry Daly who was lying at the end of her bed watching this strange behavior.

She tipped her hat slightly back on her head. "I'm Annie Oakley," she said in her best American cowgirl accent. "Ain't nobody gonna mess with me." She continued to strut around her bedroom. Nanny walked taller with every stride she took. Once again she casually turned to Henry, "Shucks Henry Daly," she said, "we gotta save Santa Claus tonight. Now ain't that somethin'?"

"It sure is Annie Oakley," replied Henry with half a smile across his snout and a soft wag of his tail, thump, thump on the bedpost again. "It sure is."

Nanny smiled back at Henry. Now that she was in the mode of her number one heroine, she was ready to put her best foot forward and get this night over with—to rescue Santa. "I do believe I'm feeling quite brave now Henry Daly. I'm anxious to get started."

Nanny didn't get a chance to practice with her magic shillelagh too often as she promised King Brian she would only use her leprechaun magic for the good of mankind and animal-kind and for no other reason. "This rescue mission would be so much easier if we could use our shillelaghs, Henry Daly." Nanny stood at ease with her left hand behind her back and her fingers crossed. She closed her eyes tightly and held out her right hand and chanted,

> "Oh shillelagh, come to me,
> And spread your twinkle dust.
> We've a mission on the horizon.
> Rescuing Santa is a must."

The top drawer of her nightstand opened. The small shillelagh King Brian gave to Nanny after their first adventure in the Banshee's Cradle spiraled itself to attention. Lilting Irish music filled the air. Nanny recognized the music from her Irish dancing class in school—it was "The Walls of Limerick."

Nanny opened her eyes to see what brought on this Irish dance music. The shillelagh leaped from the drawer of Nanny's nightstand onto Nanny's bed and danced out "The Walls of Limerick." Nanny, wide-eyed, was delighted to see the shillelagh so animated.

"My goodness, shillelagh," said Nanny, "you're as good a dancer as any of the leprechauns."

Nanny began tapping her foot and clapping her hands. The shillelagh danced in and out twice, then in a circle. It crossed over to the other side on the diagonal and landed in Nanny's hand leaving traces of twinkle dust in the air. The music continued. Nanny was so enchanted she cried, "Dance some more," and she too began to dance.

Henry sat to attention on Nanny's bed watching the shillelagh dance and Nanny giving it an encore and joining in. "Nanny sometimes does the strangest things," he said.

"La la, la la, la la la," she sang as she got into her stride. "Come on Henry Daly, stand beside me. This dance is supposed to be two opposite two, but we'll go with just the three of us."

Henry obliged and jumped from Nanny's bed. He felt and looked awkward dancing "The walls of Limerick" with four feet instead of two, but he was very happy to be dancing.

"Nanny." It was her mother. "What are you doing?"

Nanny tossed her hat, jumped into bed and covered herself quickly with the Blankets—only her auburn curly locks and her brown eyes were visible. Henry Daly leapt on the bed and pretended to be sleeping. The shillelagh played dead on the floor.

Nanny's bedroom door swung open. "What's this racket about?" quizzed her mother. It sounds to me like you have a ceili going on in here."

"Eh, I wasn't tired, so I decided to dance to make myself tired." Nanny put her hand to her mouth and yawned. "Now I'm so tired," she said.

"Why can't you be like Henry and just go to bed and go to sleep Nanny?" asked Mom as she walked her way around the bed tucking Nanny in. Henry had both eyes closed and didn't move a muscle.

Nanny's mother accidently stood on the shillelagh as she circled the bed. "What's this?" She bent down and picked up Nanny's shillelagh.

Nanny's eye's opened wide. Henry Daly continued to lay perfectly still. He thought he would let Nanny handle this one on her own.

"It's my shillelagh," answered Nanny softly.

"I know what it is," replied Nanny's mother. "What's it doing just lying there on the floor for somebody to walk on? Never mind Nanny, just go to sleep."

Mom placed the shillelagh on the nightstand, kissed Nanny on the forehead, and said, "Good night Nanny, no more shenanigans out of you." Mom then turned out Nanny's light and left the room quietly, closing the door behind her.

Nanny closed her eyes. She and Henry Daly lay without moving in the darkness for several minutes. They were both thinking the same thing: Santa, the Banshee's Cradle, the Rescueteers, and the night that lay ahead of them.

CHAPTER NINE

"I know, we got a little out of hand with the shillelagh, Henry Daly," whispered Nanny. "I just felt like dancing when I heard the music—I couldn't help myself. But now we need to get the items on our checklist together."

Nanny once again slid out of bed and softly landed on the floor. Henry lay quietly watching Nanny.

"I'm not going to make the same mistake twice," said Nanny. "I'm not using my shillelagh this time. I'll snap my fingers instead to put my checklist together."

Nanny took the list from her pocket. It was neatly folded in a perfect square. Princess Tara, acting as administrative assistant at the Rescueteers meeting had done the honors of folding Nanny's checklist for her.

"What a perfect square," said Nanny admiring the precise angles and edges of the folded checklist. "It's just like Princess Tara, neat and tidy, all tucked in and nothing sticking out."

Nanny flipped on her bedside light and stood in front of the mirror on her dresser, and for the first time took a good look at herself. Her head of untidy hair jumped out at her. Thick locks of curls stuck out at all angles and in different lengths. Nothing at all looked neat and tidy about her hair.

"Princess Tara would never have untidy hair like this, she would brush hair like mine until it straightened itself up," she said.

Nanny had an idea on how to tidy up her hair. She picked up Henry Daly's water bowl and placed it on her dresser. "I'm going to give myself straight hair right now," she said. From her dresser she removed a pair of socks, one stuffed into the other, and dipped them into the water bowl. Nanny squeezed the excess water from the socks and then dampened the hair around her ears. Her hair was spring loaded and wouldn't flatten like she wanted it too. "My hair is so stubborn, it won't go smooth." Feeling impatient, she dipped the socks again, this time she didn't squeeze the excess water out into Henry's bowl. She tilted her head to one side and squeezed the water out of the socks onto the hair around her ears and quickly stroked the socks over her wet hair like a hair brush. Then she brushed over her wet hair and it flattened.

"That's more like it," said Nanny.

Henry Daly lay on the bed with his head resting on his front paws, only his eyes moved as he watched Nanny. He was neither confused nor surprised by Nanny's actions. "More strange behavior," he said quietly.

"Now the other side," said Nanny and repeated the same successful process. She tucked her wet, flat hair behind her ears. Now both sides of her hair around her ears were neat and tidy.

She stared into the mirror at the rest of her hair. "That looks a bit strange," she said. "I have straight hair around my ears and nothing but untidy curls at the top of my head. Well, I know exactly what to do for that." She had an easy remedy for the top of her head. She put her cowboy hat on and pulled it down tight. Nanny nodded at herself in the mirror. "That did the trick."

"OK Henry Daly, here's what we need," said Nanny as she opened her list and read, "A backpack which must contain a flashlight, twenty feet of nylon rope, two bars of plain milk chocolate, two bars of dark chocolate, a sewing needle and a spool of black thread, and lastly, a tin whistle in the key of d."

Nanny placed her checklist on the floor. Again, she closed her eyes, took a deep breath and the magic words just came to her,

> "And now it's time to make a wish,
> A wish of great importance,
> Give me all on my list,
> And guarantee performance."

Nanny snapped her fingers.

This time no music filled the air, but there was a modest amount of twinkle dust.

Each item on Nanny's checklist played a vital role in Santa's rescue. Without them, they were all doomed. "I have to double-check my list Henry Daly. When we get to the Banshee's Cradle there's no looking back. Imagine something going wrong because I forgot stuff. I can't let that happen."

A strange feeling came over Nanny; she was in her Annie Oakley mode. "It's so important, Henry Daly, that we get Santa back. That's why we can't be afraid. We must resolve to do what we need to do," whispered Nanny.

Suddenly there was a tapping on Nanny's bedroom window. Henry Daly growled. Nanny didn't know whether to run and scream for her mother or to answer the window.

Tap tap tap.

"Who's there?" asked Nanny as she nervously wiped the fog from her window with the lace curtain to see more clearly. Ned's red-haired fringe and freckled face peered back at her.

"It's me, N-Ned—let-t me in." He was outside bundled up in his jacket, cowboy hat and woolen gloves, shivering, teeth chattering.

"Ned, what are you doing here?" Nanny whispered as she quietly opened the window, glancing back for a brief moment at her bedroom door.

"Why is your hair wet?" quizzed Ned as he stared at Nanny's hair behind her earlobes and noticed drops of water trickle down her neck.

"It's not wet," Nanny answered abruptly. "It's neat and tidy."

Ned frowned. Sure, she may think her hair was neat and tidy. To him, it just looked soggy and wet. And from his standpoint outside the window, her wet hair would just make her colder. This confirmed all his suspicions about girls since he started palling around with Nanny. They're just weird.

Nanny knew her mother could hear the grass grow. "If my mother hears you, I'll be in deep trouble. She was just in here—she heard Henry Daly and I dancing."

"Dancing?" exclaimed Ned. Both Ned and Henry glanced at each other, sometimes Nanny did the strangest things.

What were you dancing for?" Ned climbed in the window and blew warm breath into his hands.

"Shh, keep your voice down," answered Nanny. "The shillelagh started the dancing. I was doing my magic with it and next thing I know, the shillelagh is dancing "The Walls of Limerick" just like teacher taught us in school."

"The shillelagh?" Ned was totally bewildered. Was Nanny's shillelagh's more magical than his? "How come my shillelagh didn't do that?"

"Maybe because you don't know the dance," replied Nanny. "I think you were in the corner when we were learning that. That was in your bully days when you were in the corner all the time."

"No I wasn't," answered Ned as though he never spent any time in the corner in school. "I know how to dance "The Walls of Limerick."

"Me too," added Henry Daly with a smile. "In and out twice, then a circle and cross over to the other side."

"Who taught you that?" Ned asked Henry Daly.

"The shillelagh did," Henry answered proudly, liking being part of the dance class. "Would you like me to teach you, Ned?"

"We don't have time for dance classes now," interrupted Nanny. "We're on our way to save Santa from the Banshee or have you two forgotten?"

"No I haven't forgotten," said Ned. "That's why I'm here. Anyway I already know "The Walls of Limerick" he added with a freckle-faced frown.

Nanny had her doubts that Ned knew the dance, but if he didn't she and Henry Daly would teach it to him another time.

After spending the last several hours dwelling on the Banshee and the absolute horror of the Banshee's Cradle, Ned was ready to surrender his thoughts to Nanny. "I'm not able to eat. I can't rest, Nanny," he said. "I can't sleep and I'm sick to my stomach." He paused and took a deep breath. "I really want to be brave like you and Princess Tara," he said. "After all, I'm bigger and older."

"By three weeks," said Nanny, holding her three fingers under Ned's nose.

"I just can't find an ounce of bravery in me," continued Ned. "I'm not going Nanny. I really want to but I can't, I just can't." He dropped his head in shame.

Nanny didn't have to ask Ned why. He was afraid, and rightly so. Nanny was afraid too.

"I'm not going either," replied Nanny. "I'm afraid too."

Nanny's response took Ned by surprise. Henry Daly wore the same expression as Ned, one of shock. It was just moments before Ned showed up that Nanny had just said how they shouldn't be afraid and how they must resolve to do what they needed to do.

"But what about Santa?" said Ned. "You have to go, Nanny."

"No I don't," she answered. "Nanny Reilly was in the Banshee's Cradle once and after that she vowed she would never go back again, no matter what."

"But who's going to help rescue Santa if we don't go?" asked Ned.

Nanny turned away from Ned and began to strut slowly across her bedroom. She had her cowboy hat on. Once again she imagined her fringed cowgirl suit, her clanking spurs and the sound of her leather boots on a wooden floor. She casually turned to Ned, and tilted her hat on her head.

"Shucks Mr. Ranger," she said in her American cowgirl accent, "we gotta save Santa Claus tonight. Now ain't that somethin'?"

Ned didn't respond. He stood staring at Nanny. He thought this behavior was a fine example of Nanny being a girl, doing the strangest things.

"It sure is, Annie Oakley," answered Henry Daly. "It sure is."

"Annie Oakley," said Ned.

"Shh," said Nanny, "keep your voice down." Nanny glanced at her bedroom door again. "It's the only way I can pluck up the courage to go. When I pretend I'm Annie Oakley I feel braver. She would surely rescue Santa. So that's what I have to do to go back into the Banshee's Cradle. Nanny Reilly is staying here and Annie Oakley is going in her place."

"That's a good idea," said Ned. Perhaps Nanny's strange behavior had some merit to it. "I wonder if I pretended hard enough to be the Lone Ranger, would it help me?"

"I bet it would," said Nanny. "You did a good job at Annie Oakley today. Just do the same thing only you're the Lone Ranger. You have to practice like I did and you have to imagine."

Nanny strutted across the room again demonstrating her newfound courage. "Walk across the room like you're in walking in Dodge City with your cowboy hat, your boots, and your spurs. Imagine you just got all the bad guys to leave town and everybody is tipping their hat at you."

Ned gave his best attempt at a strut. His fear still showed as he stiffly walked across Nanny's bedroom. It wasn't very good. "It's no good Nanny," he said. "I can't do it."

"That's because you're thinking like Ned Franey," said Nanny. "Think like your hero, <u>be</u> the Lone Ranger. How does he walk in his boots and spurs? What would he do about Santa?"

Nanny got into her mode again, strutted away from Ned, slowly turned and tipped her hat. "Shucks Mr. Ranger, we gotta save Santa Claus tonight, now ain't that somethin'."

Ned relaxed his body and got into his Lone Ranger mode. He imagined himself in Dodge City, wearing his hat, his boots and spurs, and the folks around giving him admiration for all for his bravery. He strutted across the room toward Nanny. "It sure is Annie Oakley," he said in his best American cowboy accent. "It sure is."

Nanny and Henry Daly smiled a big bright smile at Ned. "You bet your bottom dollar it is Mr. Ranger. Let's show the Banshee what we're made of," replied Nanny.

Ned felt braver, maybe not quite as brave as he wanted to, but several more struts across the room would soon take care of that. Nanny too bundled up in her warm winter coat, her cowboy hat and woolen gloves. On their way out the window, Nanny glanced back at her cozy little bedroom, at her homemade Christmas decorations stretched from corner to corner. A garland of green paper Christmas trees, a garland of red paper Christmas bells, and a garland of Santa's, their beards made from cotton balls.

"Don't you worry Santa," she whispered softly. "The Rescueteers are going to find you and bring you home. We have a plan." Nanny held onto those words as she and Henry Daly quietly followed Ned out the window and headed for Magandy's Pond.

CHAPTER TEN

Santa was sitting at the edge of his cell bed with his arms folded, waiting for midnight to arrive. Then it would be Christmas Eve and he could at last make time stand still and perform a little of his own Christmas magic.

"Midnight is close, I can feel it," he said.

He stood and braced himself for the magical feeling that came over him at the stroke of midnight when Christmas Eve began. Santa described it to Mrs. Claus as an exhilarating warmth with butterflies in his bones, springs on the souls of his feet, and a smile across his face that just won't quit.

"I don't feel the magic just yet. Come on, Christmas Eve," he said, "make my spirit bright." But alas, that didn't happen. All of a sudden doom and gloom took over Santa. His body was gripped with fear, worry, despair, and defeat.

"What's happening to me?" he said as he held his stomach and fell to his knees. "There's no Christmas magic in the air. What can I do to get out of here?"

The weight of Santa's woes were so heavy, he barely managed to get to his feet. He frantically pounded the cold walls of his cell with his closed fist, looking for a loose brick. But the walls, cold and dark, were firm. He walked around looking for something, anything, to give him hope, but found nothing. There wasn't even a mouse scurrying on the stone floor to share his anxious moments with.

"This can't possibly be happening," he wailed softly. "I've had centuries of fun at the North Pole with Rudolph, Prancer, and Dancer and all my reindeers, with Mrs. Claus and all my hard-working elves who care so much about the children and love the festive season. What about all of them, what will they do without Christmas?"

Santa heard the heavy door at the top of the stairway squeak its way open. It was the Banshee. He could smell her—like rotten fruit and the sadness of being alone.

"I can't let the Banshee see me in such despair," he said. "I'll perk myself up and give myself hope." He removed his belt from his jacket and his red holly-printed handkerchief from his trouser pocket.

"How do you feel now, Mr. Santa Claus?" The Banshee was laughing as she made her way to Santa's cell. "It's Christmas Eve and you get to spend it with the greatest Banshee since time began." She held her scrawny arms out as if she would hug him. They looked like dead branches off a very old, very unhappy tree.

"Don't be too sure of that, Banshee," said Santa in his deep, calm voice. Santa blew his warm breath on his belt buckle and began to shine it with his handkerchief.

The Banshee snarled, "I hear silly people talk about their best Christmas ever, and it upsets me, but now I understand. For me, this year, it surely is the best Christmas ever, even though Christmas is last on my list for celebration."

"Banshee," said Santa, "how long have you known me?"

The Banshee paused. "Why do you ask?" Her voice wavered, as if she suspected Santa might be up to something.

"I ask because I have been around as long as you have," said Santa as he walked to his cell door. He stuffed his handkerchief back into his pocket with a casual hand, then stared the Banshee in the eye. "And have you ever known me to miss a Christmas?" Santa asked, forcing a laugh into his voice.

"Not until now," answered the Banshee laughing. "There are too many happy people. You get great satisfaction out of seeing delight in people at Christmas—I get great satisfaction out of seeing despair in people at Christmas. Hours from now, Christmas cheer will be a thing of the past, ha ha ha. Just think of all the people, young and old, who will be so disappointed when Santa ignores them all. No more Merry Christmas," she laughed wickedly. "Your old magical self no longer exists. I have stopped Christmas, so there's no point in shining your belt.

The only place you're going is to departures, where all my new recruits go, and a shiny belt won't do you any good there."

"You underestimate the powers of the universe, Banshee," replied Santa in his deep soothing voice. "Christmas will always be because it's meant to be. An energy of peace and goodwill finds its way into the heart and soul of mankind. It spreads throughout the world and Christmas prevails. Try as you will, but you can't stop that."

Once again the Banshee became doubtful of her plans. With a wicked frown and without saying a word, she quickly turned. She left Santa and a cloud of dust behind her as she traveled to her lair to double check her perfect plans.

CHAPTER ELEVEN

Nanny, Ned, and Henry Daly were off once again on a midnight mission. Bertie and Frosty were eager to get started. Frosty's white coat glittered in the moonlight. The ponies were tethered to a large chestnut tree outside Nanny's bedroom window. They snorted and pawed at the ground.

"We're going on a very important mission tonight, Frosty," said Nanny. "You and Bertie are going to fly us back to the Banshee's Cradle. I hope you ate all your dinner. King Brian said you're going to need every ounce of energy you have in you for this one."

In response to Nanny, Frosty nuzzled at Nanny's face then smelled her wet hair. "Bertie, did you hear what Nanny just said?" continued Ned." A very important mission. We're the Rescueteers and we've been called by King Brian to save Santa tonight." Ned had strutted his way into a courageous mode. His fear appeared to be gone.

Nanny pulled her backpack on, strapping it good and tight. Then she scrambled her way onto Frosty's back. It was a bit of a struggle because of her thick coat and backpack, they made her feel like a snowman herself, but Frosty didn't complain and stood perfectly still for Nanny. The warmth from Frosty's back was a welcome feeling for Nanny, it took the nighttime chill out of her bones.

Ned grabbed Bertie's mane and swung himself up on his back. He looked at Nanny and tipped his hat. "Where would the Lone Ranger be without his horse Silver?" he smiled.

"And Annie Oakley without hers," replied Nanny, smiling back at Ned.

Henry Daly was alert and ready to go. He stood to attention at Frosty's feet with his head held high, his ears pricked and his tail high in the air, just anxious to get going.

He backed up, dragging his front paws in the dirt and squatting down on his to back legs. "I'm ready to go," he said, as he looked directly into Nanny's eyes.

"All right Henry Daly," said Nanny. "You lead the way." Nanny lifted her reins and gently asked Frosty to follow Henry Daly down Katie's lane. Ned and Bertie rode by their side.

Henry trotted down Katie's moonlit lane with his nose high in the air. His tail was curled up and almost touching his spine. He looked to the left, and then he looked to the right. Occasionally the trees on either side of the lane would hide the moonlight and darkness would set in. Every hundred yards or so Henry Daly stopped to smell the still night air and look behind him.

"I have to watch out for that Banshee," he said, "especially in the shadows. If she shows up, I'm going to grab her by the nose and shake her up and down, around and around, then inside out and upside down, and around and around again." It was his job to watch out for Nanny and Ned and to protect them from any kind of danger.

They came to the end of the lane. The limbs from several tall oak trees blocked the moonlit sky. It was really dark in the shadows. A glow from the moonlight shone on the gate to Katie's field, it was wide open. Henry Daly stopped dead in his tracks.

"Something's not right, the gate is open." He growled and hackles stood up on his back.

"What is it Henry Daly?" whispered Nanny.

"I'm not sure yet," answered Henry, sticking his nose high in the air and sniffing all around. "Shh, there's somebody coming. Quickly, let's hide in the shadows."

Nanny and Ned moved Bertie and Frosty quietly and quickly against the ditch and hid in the shadows of the trees. They could hear the sound of footsteps getting closer and closer. Henry Daly was on high alert. He bravely stood in front of Nanny and Ned.

Nothing scared him. He was ready to tussle with any kind of predator who threatened Nanny, Ned, or their ponies. As the sound of the footsteps got closer, they could hear somebody humming what sounded like a Christmas song.

"It sounds like a man," whispered Nanny, "and he's humming 'Santa Claus is coming to town.' Listen."

Both Ned and Henry tilted their heads to one side to listen carefully. Sure enough, they recognized the tune as they had been singing it themselves all week long.

"Hmm…hmm hmm hmm," hummed the unknown shadow.

"It smells like Bull Cullen," whispered Henry Daly as he sniffed the still night air continuously. "He's at the gate—now, keep still."

The burly shadow of large man came through the gate and then closed it behind him. He looked over his shoulder in the direction of Nanny, Ned, and Henry Daly. He held that position for a good ten seconds. Nanny and Ned kept quiet. The man moved his head as if he was trying to focus in on something.

"Ah ha," he exclaimed. "I see you. I bet you thought you could slip my eye." He took a step forward and ducked under a low hanging limb of one of the oak trees. He stretched his long thick arm out toward the ditch and with his big right hand he snapped off a piece of holly from a nice thick holly bush. "This will be perfect for my present to Santa," he chuckled. He then turned and continued on down Katie's lane. As he walked out of the shadow of the trees into the moonlight, he put his hands in his trouser pockets and began humming again. He walked with a spring in his step to the beat of the same tune, 'Santa Claus is coming to town.'

"Well, that was a surprise encounter," said Nanny.

"It surely was," sighed Ned, remembering their last unpleasant fiasco with Bull Cullen. He scared the living daylights out of them as he chased after them. Fortunately, and thanks to Henry Daly's ferocious fearlessness, he didn't catch them.

"I wonder what he was doing in Katie's field?" said Nanny. "He seemed very jolly."

"I know what he was doing," answered Henry Daly, who was already at the other side of the gate and in Katie's field. "Come and see this."

The moon shined brightly down on a lone four foot tall pine tree. A homemade silver star sat on top of the tree. Silver- and gold-wrapped candies were individually tied to the tree with multi-colored shiny streamer ribbons.

Nanny and Ned entered Katie's field, dismounted from their ponies, and closed the gate behind them. They walked over to the little Christmas tree in awe.

"It's all lit up said Ned and it doesn't even have any lights."

"It doesn't need any lights," smiled Nanny. "The moonlight is making everything shine." Nanny knelt down beside the tree and saw an old shoe box. There was a note attached to it. "To all the leprechauns of Coolrainy," she read. "Merry Christmas. I give to you my prized possession as I no longer have use for it. Your new friend, Bull Cullen.

"Imagine Bull Cullen wishing the leprechauns a Merry Christmas and giving them his prized possession ," said Ned. "Not too long ago he was trying to capture them for the Banshee."

"I'm sure all the leprechauns will be as surprised as we are," replied Nanny. "I wonder what his prized possession is."

"It must be in that box. Nanny, do you think we should take a quick look?" asked Ned.

"I don't think we should," said Nanny. "It's not for us, it's for the leprechauns."

Nanny studied the box, the temptation was hard to resist. She picked it up and gave it a little shake and then tilted it up and down. "It's not very heavy and it sounds like just one thing that's too small for the box because it's sliding up and down."

"Let me have a shake," said Ned. Ned kept his ear close to the box as he gave it a gentle shake. Then he tilted the box up and down. "I think I know what it is."

"What is it?" asked Nanny.

"I bet it's a leprechaun trap," answered Ned.

Immediately Nanny thought Ned was right. He's good at guessing gifts. He was right about the boots and spurs and he was right about King Brian wanting a fine cowboy hat like theirs.

"We should leave something for the leprechauns for Christmas," said Nanny.

"Like what?" said Ned. "We don't have anything."

Nanny searched around in her pockets. Ned was wondering what Nanny could possibly have to give the leprechauns. Fish hooks? Catgut? What did she have? He knew he didn't have a thing.

Nanny opened her fist to show Ned what her gift to the leprechauns would be.

"Your chainyalleys," he said. "But you just won them, and it took you the whole school year. Everybody was trying to win them." In fact, Ned stood close to Nanny as she played for them. He wanted Tommy Riordan to know that Nanny was his friend and there would be none of his usual shenanigans or he would have to deal with Ned Franey.

"Are you sure, Nanny?"

"Yes, I'm sure," answered Nanny as she removed a piece of the tissue paper from her fish hooks and wrapped her prized possessions in it. She placed her gift beside Bull Cullen's under the four foot tall fir tree.

Ned emptied his pockets and spread everything out on the dewy grass. He had a gold whistle carefully tucked away in a black velvet pouch. He too had fish hooks wrapped in tissue paper, jack stones, marbles, cat gut, floats made from ice pop sticks and four horse nuts, two for Bertie and two for Frosty. There was one item amongst his treasures although it was worn and slightly tattered he kept it wrapped in cellophane. He picked it up, stared at it and thought hard. Nanny looked at Ned knowing how hard it was for him to part with it.

"Are you sure, Ned?" she asked. "You've had that for as long as I've known you."

"Yes I'm sure," answered Ned. He placed his prized possession beside Nanny's under the tiny Christmas tree. "I'll be happy to see this tree again. At least then we'll know we're on our way home," he smiled.

Nanny smiled with him. At that moment she had great admiration for Ned. "Let's make a pact right here at Bull Cullen's Christmas tree," she said.

"What kind of a pact?" asked Ned.

"Let's promise to be the best and bravest Rescueteers we can be," said Nanny.

Nanny, Ned, and Henry Daly placed their hands and paws on top of each other and made their pact. At that very moment two of the bravest children in Ireland and the bravest dog looked each other in the eye, all fear aside—they knew what had to be done.

They mounted their ponies again and took a moment to stare at the lone little Christmas tree all aglow in the quiet of the moonlight in Katie's field. What a sight for them to behold with the three gifts underneath it: Bull Cullen's box, Nanny's chainyalleys, and Ned's cellophane wrapped picture card of his lifelong idol, the Lone Ranger.

CHAPTER TWELVE

At Magandy's Pond the newly recruited Rescueteers were already mounted on their miniature horses and waiting with King Brian for Nanny, Ned, and Henry Daly to arrive. Princess Tara was seated behind King Rory on his grey mare. King Brian was staring off toward Katie's field, quietly battling with his mind.

"You look worried, Brian," said King Brendan softly. "It must be Nanny and Ned you're concerned about. The Banshee in our entire lifetime has never caused you to be concerned for too long."

"Aye," answered King Brian as he dropped his head in shame. "I roped them into this mess. If I hadn't have been a mean old leprechaun king, I'd never have tricked Nanny Reilly into kidnapping my lovely niece Princess Tara. Both Nanny and Ned would be in their beds quietly sleeping with not a care in the world and we would have to find a way to rescue Santa without them."

"But you can't think like that, Brian," continued King Brendan. "Look what meeting you has done for Nanny Reilly. She and Ned were once arch enemies, they're now the best of friends. Henry Daly, Nanny's beloved dog, can talk. All three have magical powers that fortunately, they only use for the good of mankind and animal kind. Not to mention their magical ponies Bertie and Frosty, who are the center of their universe."

"And—" added Princess Tara, who was always alert to her peers and her surroundings. She slid from the back of her dad's grey mare and walked to King Brian in her usual authoritative fashion with her hand on her hip. "Look what meeting Nanny Reilly has done for you.

You're no longer a mean old leprechaun king. You're now a caring and kind king."

"You flatter me, my little niece," smiled King Brian as his cheeks blushed a rosy red. Compliments were a rarity for him especially in days of old.

King Brendan said, "It's when they're under real pressure that their true colors will shine through. If they show up tonight, they're meant to be here because they want to be and because they really care," continued the caring king.

"I suppose you're right, Brother Brendan," sighed King Brian. He was quietly hoping Nanny and Ned would find the ounce of courage they needed, even to get them to Magandy's Pond. His white horse pricked his ears and looked in the direction of Katie's field. King Brian smiled, quietly elated to see Nanny and Ned trot toward them on their ponies in the moonlight with old faithful, Henry Daly leading the way. He was so proud of them, he shed a simple tear.

Greetings were given to each other as Nanny, Ned, and Henry Daly lined up beside their associates. The moment for their daunting mission had come.

"Do you have the chocolate bars in your backpack, Nanny Reilly?" asked King Brian with a broad smile, still thrilled at the sight of Nanny and Ned.

"Yes I do," answered Nanny." I have two kinds: milk chocolate and dark chocolate."

"Good lass, Nanny Reilly," said King Brian. "Let the show begin." He reached for his shillelagh from under his cloak, pointed it at Nanny's backpack and said,

"Oh chocolate bars,
Bittersweet,
Whoever will eat
Shall fall asleep.
Oh chocolate bars,
Dark and plain,
You set the stage
For us to reign."

"How about the needle and thread Nanny Reilly, you have them with you, right?" chuckled King Brian. He was thoroughly enjoying the moment for several reasons. Nanny and Ned being there and of course preparing to outsmart the wicked Banshee one more time. Hopefully for the last time.

"Yes I do," answered Nanny with a smile.

King Brian once again pointed his shillelagh at Nanny's backpack and said,

> "Before dawn awakes the land,
> And the Banshee has the upper hand.
> Rise and shine needle and thread,
> Sew the Banshee to her bed."

"You're having too much fun, Brian," laughed King Brendan.

"I just get a little extra satisfaction out of my shillelagh when it involves surprising the Banshee," answered King Brian, with a grin. "Why don't you do the honors with the tin whistle, Brother Brendan?"

"It would be my pleasure," replied King Brendan as he reached for his shillelagh from beneath his cloak. "Nanny Reilly," he said, "do you have the tin whistle with you?"

"Yes I do," answered Nanny. "I've a tin whistle in the key of 'd'." She was proud of herself for having the exact key requested.

It was a good thing Princess Tara paid strict attention to everything and wrote the proper key down for Nanny, otherwise it would be possible the tin whistle you see is the one you'd get.

"Good lass, Nanny Reilly," smiled King Brendan. "The sound of a tin whistle in the key of 'd' will travel far and wide." He then pointed his shillelagh at Nanny's backpack and said,

> "Oh magic whistle,
> Straight and tall.
> Sure you're the sweetest
> of them all.
> With your lilting tunes
> Of carols bright,
> Help us guide Santa

Home tonight.
As dawn awakes
Stand upright
And play your tune,
"Silent Night."

"Well said, Brother Brendan," said King Cormac. "You flatter all of us."

"When it's for a good cause, it's always nice to put your best foot forward," replied King Brendan with a chuckle.

All the Rescueteers smiled and nodded in agreement. Nanny, Ned, and Henry Daly reflected on their pact. They were going to put their best foot forward and be the best and bravest Rescueteers they could be.

Ned was still quietly practicing his Lone Ranger routine in his mind. He was repeating over and over, "Shucks, Annie Oakley, we're going to save Santa Claus tonight. Now ain't that somethin'?" "Shucks Annie Oakley, we're going to save Santa Claus tonight. Now ain't that somethin'?" He really wanted to stay in the right frame of mind, and that was the only way he could do it.

"Is everybody ready?" asked King Brian. He noticed Nanny and Ned getting a little tense, although they appeared to be a whole lot more relaxed than earlier that afternoon. Perhaps the seeds of bravery have taken root and sprouted. He certainly hoped so. "Rest assured," he said to them, "sure, we'll be back in no time at all."

Nanny and Ned liked hearing those words, "we'll be back in no time at all." How comforting they were. Nanny slid her thumbs under the shoulder straps of her backpack, securing it on her back. She then patted Frosty's neck and picked up her reins. She looked at Ned and Henry Daly, giving them a tight-lipped smile. All the Rescueteers glanced around at each other with the same tight-lipped expression.

King Brian raised his right arm high in the air and cried, "Onward Rescueteers, up, up and away, to the Banshee's Cradle we go." He then asked his white horse to go forward. With a single bound, King Brian was now cantering upwards toward the starry sky, followed by King Rory on his grey horse, King Cormac on his black horse, and King Brendan on his spirited chestnut mare.

Princess Tara had swung herself up on Henry Daly's back and the greyhound leaped forward into the air. "Up, up and away, to the Banshee's Cradle we go," he bayed.

Nanny and Ned took off together on Bertie and Frosty cantering into the air. "Up, up and away, to the Banshee's Cradle we go," they cried.

The Rescueteers silhouetted the moonlit sky soaring higher and higher over the dunes, then over the shimmering ocean, and finally the thick forest.

The four kings had big, bright smiles on their faces. Riding their horses into the night sky brought back many of their own childhood memories.

King Rory rode his horse up beside King Brian. "Are you thinking what I'm thinking, Brian?" he said.

"Indeed I am, Brother Rory," answered King Brian. He looked over his shoulder and saw King Brendan and King Cormac making their way up beside them.

"I think all four of us are on the same page," chuckled King Cormac as the four brothers rode side-by-side in the night sky.

"Well, what are we waiting for?" said King Brendan as he gathered up his reins. All four kings got into the jockey stance. "After you, Brother Brian."

King Brian took off on his white horse higher and higher into the sky laughing heartily, as did King Rory, King Brendan and King Cormac.

"Over the moon and under the stars," they all shouted together. They rode their horses single file up and down in serpentine loops in the sky. Each time they reached the peak of the loop they got butterflies and yelled, "Over the moon." As they made their descent and reached the valley of the loop, they got butterflies again and yelled, "Under the stars."

Nanny, Ned, and Henry Daly with Princess Tara on his back watched all the fun and they could hear the laughter from the four kings.

"I want to play over the moon and under the stars too," said Nanny, without hesitation she picked up her reins and asked Frosty to catch up and follow behind King Cormac.

"Me too," said Ned. "We may as well have a little fun. What do you think, Henry Daly?"

"I'm all for it if Princess Tara is," answered Henry.

"Count me in," said Princess Tara. "This is the first time all my uncles and my dad have had fun on their horses in a very long time. I want to share in the fun with them."

"That's all I need to hear," said Henry Daly as he, Ned, and Princess Tara joined the ride of a lifetime.

"Over the moon," yelled all the Rescueteers together at the peaks, getting butterflies galore of course. "Under the stars," they all yelled in unison at the valleys.

For several minutes, the Banshee seemed to be far from their minds as laughter and joy filled the moonlit starry sky at the early hours of Christmas Eve on the way to rescue Santa Claus.

CHAPTER THIRTEEN

King Brian finally led the ride back down toward the forest. The smiles and laughter stopped. The lush pine tree scent filled the air as they finally made their descent to the outskirts of the Banshee's Cradle where they couldn't be detected by any of the Banshee's skeleguards or evil devices.

The forest floor was covered in pine needles, pine cones, twigs and some fallen branches. The landing had to be quiet. The skeleguards would be alerted if they heard anything unusual. The landing had been discussed at the meeting the afternoon before at Magandy's Pond, so with extreme caution, the group landed in an open area where there were little or no noisy twigs and pine needles scattered about.

Nanny and Ned quietly tethered Bertie and Frosty to a low branch of a pine tree. "Are you okay, Ned?" whispered Nanny with a nervous quiver in her voice.

"Shucks, Annie Oakley," said Ned in a nervous whisper, "we're going to rescue Santa Claus tonight. Now ain't that somethin'?"

"It sure is, Mr. Ranger," answered Nanny with a quiver. "It sure is."

The four kings dismounted and ground tied their horses.

Princess Tara leaned forward and gave Henry Daly a big hug. "Thank you, Henry Daly," she whispered as she quietly slid from his back. Henry Daly smiled bashfully. He gently bowed his head and whispered his reply. "You're very welcome, Princess Tara."

"Gather round," said King Brian quietly as he gestured with both hands for the Rescueteers to come closer to him. "This is as close as we can get to the Banshee's Cradle without been seen or heard. All our magic powers stop ten yards from this site. As soon as we cross that line we'll be surviving on our wits alone. But first let's make sure, just to be sure."

King Brian quietly stepped out ten yards. He took out his shillelagh and waved it in small circles.

"May our leprechaun magic
Break the wish-blocking device,
May Santa Claus appear
And be within our sights."

The Rescueteers held their breath and crossed their fingers. The ferns and grass before King Brian began to rustle as a misty fog arose. Could Santa possibly be appearing? Then, just as their hopes were getting high, the ferny grass withered and slowly died, leaving a patch of dead and dried out foliage amidst the lush green surroundings.

"Saints preserve us," said King Brian. "Now we have an idea of what the whole of Ireland could look like if the Banshee has her way. Is everybody ready?" King Brian looked all the Rescueteers in the eye for the nod of readiness. "All right then," he chuckled, spitting on the palms of both hands and rubbing them together. "Let's shake up the Banshee a little bit."

"I'm not looking forward to this," said King Brendan. He had a satchel of six- inch wooded stakes strapped over his shoulder, which were quite sizeable and heavy for King Brendan considering he was only ten inches tall. He took a small hammer from under his cloak and held it up at eye level. "It has been a while since we've bewildered the Banshee, Brian."

"Well, in that case, Brother Brendan," answered King Brian, "let's show her what we're made of." King Brian removed his cloak and carefully folded it. He then handed it to Nanny. Nanny removed her backpack from her back and put King Brian's tiny cloak in it.

"All right Nanny Reilly, Ned Franey and Henry Daly, are you ready for round one?" asked King Brian.

"We're ready," answered the three together. Nanny and Ned took a deep breath. Ned put his hand in his pocket to hold onto his Lone

Ranger picture card, forgetting he left it at the foot of Bull Cullen's Christmas tree. Nanny recognized his reach and knew he badly wanted to hold onto the picture of his lifelong hero. She grabbed his hand.

"Boots and spurs on a wooden floor," she whispered to him.

Ned squeezed Nanny's hand acknowledging her words. "We have our checklist and we know what to do," he replied as he gave Nanny a reassuring nod.

"Now remember, Henry Daly," smiled King Brian as he put his finger to his lips, "no talking."

"Don't you worry," answered Henry Daly in his scratchy voice. "My secret is safe with me, and I promise I won't let myself get separated from Nanny and Ned."

Nanny's and Ned's hearts were pounding as they quietly followed Henry Daly and made their way to the gates of the Banshee's Cradle. The remaining Rescueteers closely watched from behind a cluster of lush green ferns. They were up next. Henry was not frightened at all, just cautious. Nanny and Ned carefully placed one foot in front of the other, taking small precise steps. Nanny's backpack was on her back with all her checklist items. She held on tightly to it with both thumbs under the shoulder straps and her sweating fists tightly clenched. Everything going well depended on what was in her backpack, Henry Daly keeping his secret, and herself and Ned staying focused.

Henry stopped and looked back at Nanny and Ned. "We're here," he softly whispered.

Nanny, Ned, and Henry Daly lay down and concealed themselves behind some ferns and tall grass. They stared straight ahead of them. It was a scary sight. There it was, the Banshee's Cradle, looking even more daunting than it did before. They could see four skeleguards, who were alert and waiting for any intruders, just like the leprechaun scout had reported to King Brian. Two skeleguards patrolled the perimeter of the Cradle while two remained at the south entrance gates. The skeleguards at the gates had a skeledog at their sides.

Time was of the essence, so Nanny, Ned, and Henry Daly made their move. They crawled on their stomachs through the ferny grass to the west side of the Banshee's Cradle and waited for the patrolling skeleguard to pass. It would be six minutes before he was back.

As the skeleguard disappeared behind the north wall, all three ran as fast as they could to the west wall. Henry was the first to reach their destination. Nanny was three strides behind him.

When they reached the wall, Nanny removed her backpack and took the twenty-foot rope out, she turned to Ned, but he wasn't there. Where was Ned?

"Ned, Ned," said Nanny in a loud whisper as she frantically began looking around her. "Where are you?" Henry was showing all his teeth, growling ferociously, his hackles up on his back. Two skeleguards were walking toward them with Ned by the scruff of the neck. Ned was trying to punch them, but his arms were just swinging wildly while the skeleguards laughed at him.

"I'm sorry Nanny," said Ned, almost in tears. "They were hiding in the brush waiting for us. Then they just pounced on me while I was running behind you and I couldn't get away."

The blood drained from Nanny's face. "Now what do we do?" She too was almost in tears.

"Surprise, surprise," said one of the skeleguards to Nanny. "The Banshee knew you lot would try and sneak in to the Cradle. We just hid and waited for you. There's no escaping us this time."

Henry Daly continued growling. He stood tight against Nanny's side.

"Keep that dog quiet," yelled one of the skeleguards at Nanny, "or I'll permanently shut him up for you. We could do with another skeledog around here, ha ha ha."

"Please be quiet, Henry Daly," said Nanny as she knelt beside Henry and hugged him. Under severe protest, Henry stopped growling.

"Let's get these three sillies to the Banshee before we take them to departures," laughed the other skeleguard. "The Banshee will be really pleased with us and we'll surely win Skeleguard of the Month."

Nanny and Ned were trembling.

"Ned," said Nanny as tears rolled down her face. "I didn't think I could feel so scared."

"Me neither, Nanny," sobbed Ned. He didn't want Nanny to feel as scared as he felt, but he couldn't do anything about it.

"All we can do now is hope for the best." Nanny put her backpack back in order and put it on her back, then stood and held Henry Daly by the collar. Henry Daly showed no sign of fear. He was bothered by the skeleguards' treatment of Ned. They better not yank Nanny around like that, so he continued to snarl and show his sharp canine teeth. Henry really wanted to tell the skeleguards what he was going to do with them if they hurt his comrades, but he couldn't let them know he could talk. This was a lot more difficult than he thought it was going to be. Nanny and Ned tightly held hands while they were marched back along the west side wall to the main gates, which were now wide open awaiting their arrival.

CHAPTER FOURTEEN

The Banshee was sitting at her dusty cluttered desk in her boudoir sifting through her 'New Arrivals' list. She was looking for King Brian's name. "He has not checked in yet. There will be a new list tonight, he will surely be on that. King Brian of Coolrainy will finally be on my guest list. I'll make sure I'll give him VIP treatment, ha ha ha," she laughed.

A loud knock came to her door, <u>knock</u>, <u>knock</u>, <u>knock</u>. "This better be good," was the Banshee's angry reply. "Everybody knows by now not to disturb the Banshee in her boudoir, it's for my most private secret things."

She stood quickly from her desk knocking over her skelechair. She stormed to the door leaving a cloud of dust behind her as she viciously swung the door open and leaned her whole body forward, an angry frown on her face. The Banshee was ready to yell at whoever was at the door. Suddenly her expression changed. A broad smile came across her bony, wart-infested face. Her pointed chin almost touched the tip of her long hook nose. She had no teeth. It was hard to tell if she even had gums. There standing in front of the Banshee, were two broad smiling skeleguards, in front of them was, Nanny Reilly, Ned Franey, and Henry Daly.

"Well now, who do we have here?" said the Banshee in the sweetest, most beautiful voice she could come up with, although it didn't sound sweet or beautiful to the recipients. "Two silly children and a silly dog. Are you the same two silly children and silly dog who dared to invade the Banshee's Cradle on a summer eve?"

Nanny and Ned took a step back. Henry Daly took a step forward and snarled at the Banshee. He sniffed the air, smelling the Banshee's moldy black attire. The Banshee's grey hair seemed to take over her head, she had a lot of it.

"We were on a r-r-rescue m-m-mission," stammered Ned.

Nanny quickly nudged Ned with her elbow. "We just got lost," continued Nanny.

"Grr," growled Henry Daly.

"Spare me your pathetic reasons," answered the Banshee as she squinted her eyes and leaned into Nanny's face. Nanny got a close up of the Banshee's hairy warts on her nose. "Nobody comes on a rescue mission into the Banshee's Cradle and gets away with it, and nobody gets lost and wanders into the Banshee's Cradle."

Henry's fierce growling and snarling didn't affect the Banshee in any way. She was well used to angry traits. Howling, growling and snarling sounds were just a common background noise and normal to her.

"We're very sorry Banshee," said Ned nervously. "May we go home now?"

"Go home?" laughed the Banshee. "Don't be ridiculous. This is your home now, ha ha ha." The two skeleguards laughed with the Banshee. "And I have another vacancy for that silly leprechaun king," added the Banshee. "I'll soon be sending you all to skeleresources with Mr. Santa Claus to get you registered and on my skelelist, ha ha ha. This is too good."

The Banshee's laugh got louder and stronger. The skeleguard's teeth clattered together in laughter. Nanny and Ned cowered down with their hands over their ears. The laughter from the Banshee and the skeleguards was a frightening sound. Henry Daly growled louder and longer.

"Now where is that silly leprechaun king?" continued the Banshee. "I'm sure he's close by."

The Banshee began sniffing the air all around Nanny, her nose crinkled up, it moved left and right, then up and down. It torpedoed in on Nanny's backpack. The Banshee stood up straight and smiled. "Give it to me," she said to Nanny as she stretched out her bony hand gesturing to Nanny to put her backpack in her hand.

Nanny reluctantly removed her backpack. She handed it to the Banshee and dropped her head in sorrow. So too did Ned. Henry Daly made no movement, but continued growling.

The Banshee pressed Nanny's backpack against her nose with both her long finger-nailed bony hands. She inhaled as much as she possibly could, held her breath for a few seconds and then exhaled.

"Fee fo fi fum. I always wanted to say that, ha ha ha," she laughed. "Oh come out come out wherever you are," she sang. "I always wanted to sing that too." She laughed heartlessly, ha ha ha. "Knock, knock," she said. "Who's there?" she answered. She paused for a brief moment as though she was expecting an answer. Then she tore open Nanny's backpack, turned it upside down and shook out the contents. Nanny's checklist of items fell out together with King Brian's cloak.

"Chocolate bars," said the Banshee staring at the items in disbelief, "a stupid tin whistle, a rope, a flashlight and a needle and thread." She was really expecting King Brian to hit the floor.

The Banshee peered into the backpack. It was empty. She bent over a quickly snatched up King Brian's cloak. She held it tightly in her fist and shook it in front of Nanny's face. The Banshee's smile was now gone.

"Where is he?" she demanded.

Once again the Banshee's beady eyes were squinting and Nanny now had another close up of the Banshee's hairy warts.

"He's still outside the Cradle," quickly answered Ned as he took half a step forward and stood a little in front of Nanny. Nanny took a step sideways and stood behind Ned's shoulder. She'd had enough of the close up of the Banshee's warty nose and toothless gums.

The Banshee stared at Ned. She tightened her lips and leaned into him. Now it was Ned's turn to get a close up of her nose. Even though Ned was terrified of being so close to the scary, ugly, intimidating Banshee and he really wanted to turn and run, he stood his ground with his fists clenched. Henry Daly's teeth were still showing as he continued growling.

"Take them to join our guest of honor," the Banshee said to the skeleguards, as she stood up straight. Then I want you to find that stupid, silly, ridiculous, slimy leprechaun king. He's here somewhere, either inside, or outside the Cradle. I know he's planning to be here, and when he does I'm ready for him." Once again the Banshee glared at Ned. Ned swallowed hard. He was about to say something else, but Nanny nudged him hard.

"May I have my backpack back?" asked Nanny as she stretched out her hand. Nanny lips were quivering as she spoke. She really wanted to cry, but the Banshee would only laugh at her and stick her ugly nose in Nanny's face again.

"No, you may not," replied the Banshee angrily. "It's no longer your backpack, it is <u>mine</u>. Everything in the Banshee's Cradle is <u>mine</u>, <u>mine</u>, <u>mine</u>." Then her voice softened. "Even you, Nanny Reilly." Nanny quickly pulled back her hand. She certainly didn't like to hear the Banshee say Nanny was hers.

"Not for long," Nanny thought, "not for long."

"But we have nothing to eat," said Ned, "and I'm hungry. The dark chocolate is mine and the milk chocolate is Nanny's."

"Nobody eats chocolate bars in the Banshee's Cradle," snapped the Banshee. "Nobody except me, that is." She gathered up the bars of chocolate, and pressed them against her nose. She inhaled the chocolate aroma. "Ah," she sighed, "milk chocolate and dark chocolate, my two earthly pleasures. I must keep these safe." The Banshee put the bars in her gown pocket.

"May I have my tin whistle back?" asked Nanny as she extended her hand again.

"Some children never learn," replied the Banshee in her wicked raspy voice. She began picking up all the fallen items and putting them in the backpack. "Nothing in this backpack is yours anymore, ever. The tin whistle is mine now. Mine, mine, mine. So are the rope and flashlight, the needle and thread and this stupid-looking cloak."

Nanny stood her ground, she tightened her lips, dropped her head, and frowned. "The Banshee really is a mean old witch. I can't wait to see the back of her," she thought.

The Banshee was getting irritated with Nanny, Ned, and Henry Daly. She thought they talked too much and were too stupid not to be as scared as she would like them to be. "Take these two and that silly growling dog out of my sight," said the Banshee. "Put them with our other guest. I have more important things to deal with. We must find that stupid leprechaun king. He's more trouble than these three put together."

Her face tightened with anger as she returned to her boudoir and slammed the heavy wooden door behind her.

Nanny, Ned, and Henry Daly were escorted down the dark and dusty corridor. This was worse than they could have ever imagined. They weren't strutting now. They disappeared into the darkness and out of sight.

CHAPTER FIFTEEN

King Brian, King Brendan, King Rory, King Cormac and Princess Tara watched from behind the ferns as Nanny, Ned, and Henry Daly were taken by the skeleguards and the gates of the Banshee's Cradle closed behind them. Though it was hard to watch, they thought they really were the two bravest children in Ireland, and the bravest dog to put themselves in that position for all the children of the world. King Brian dropped his head into his hands and silently questioned his invincible plan. Now it was up to them, the leprechaun contingent, to keep their wits about them and get Nanny, Ned, and Henry Daly out of captivity, not forgetting Santa Claus, of course.

Meanwhile, Santa was standing at his cell door listening to the laughs of the Banshee. He could also hear other laughter with hers. What could possibly be going on up there? Santa had no idea it was the skeleguards laughing with the Banshee at Nanny, Ned and Henry Daly. Then he heard a door slamming and the scuffling of more than just one pair of feet in the corridor above him.

"Come on, move it, and shut that dog up," he heard as the thick wooden door creaked its way open at the top of the stairs.

"I believe I'm going to have some company on Christmas Eve after all," Santa said as he tried to get a visual on the new arrivals. "I wonder who the poor unfortunates are who had the bad misfortune of being caught by the Banshee?" But it was too dark at the top of the stairs to see anybody clearly. Try as he might, Santa just saw outlines of what seemed to be two very short people and possibly a growling dog.

Nanny was first in line coming down the steep steps of the dark stairwell. She had one hand on the wall to help her with her balance and one hand on Henry Daly's collar. The wall felt cold and moist. At the end of the stairway, a bat hung upside down below a dimly lit candle. Other than that glimmer of light there was no light at all on the stairs.

Ned too had one hand on the wall as he focused on each step. He was quietly sobbing. "I'm so scared Nanny," he said.

"I know Ned," answered Nanny, "me too. I've never been so scared in all my life. I really, really, want to go home."

"Did you not hear the Banshee?" said one of the skeleguards. "This is your home now, the Banshee's Cradle, ha ha ha." Both skeleguards laughed hard again.

Now they were at the end of the stairs and they could see Santa in his dimly lit cell squinting and looking over the rim of his gold glasses to see who was approaching. Santa's eyes opened wide in disbelief when he saw two children and a dog being ushered by the skeleguards toward his cell.

"Children," he said in shock. "Here? On Christmas Eve? That's despicable." He grabbed his cell bars and shook them hard.

"Easy there, Mr. Santa Claus," said the skeleguard. "Stand back against the wall and don't try anything funny or your co-pilots here will make an early departure, ha ha ha." They both laughed again, and their teeth chattered as they did so.

Santa had no choice, his concern now was not of himself, but of the two children and the dog who stood before him. All he could do was step back against the wall of his cell and watch the two skeleguards open the his cell door and usher a terrified Nanny and Ned and a growling Henry Daly in.

"Here's an opportunity to tell Santa what you want for Christmas," joked one of the skeleguards. "We would love to stay and join the party but like the Banshee, we have more important things to deal with."

The skeleguards high fived each other, thrilled with their capture of Nanny, Ned, and Henry Daly. They felt sure they were getting skeleguards of the month, possibly even skeleguards of the year for this one. They marched away in a hurry and clattered their way back up the dark, dingy stairway. King Brian was on their mind, he was their next target.

A warm feeling suddenly came over Nanny and Ned. There standing before them was Santa Claus. He was tall and burly with rosy red cheeks. He had white hair and a white beard. A pair of half-rimmed glasses with a gold frame sat on the bridge of his nose. He didn't have his Santa hat on, but he did have a long red cloak with white trim and a hood. Under his cloak was a long red jacket with a black belt and fur boots up to his knees. He had a leather pouch attached to his belt.

He looked down at them over the rim of his glasses and smiled a warm comforting smile. They now felt safe.

CHAPTER SIXTEEN

"Are you ready, Brother Brendan?" whispered King Brian.

"I'm as ready as I'll ever be," answered King Brendan. He then removed his cloak and handed it to King Brian. He held up his little hammer. "Sure where would we be without the tools of the trade, Brian? Wish me luck," he said as he winked at King Brian and took off toward the Banshee's Cradle at a slow pace. The wooden stakes were heavy and weighing him down a little so he stopped behind the ferns and tall grass on his way to take a breather, and also to stay out of sight. He made it to the east wall without being seen, and there he stood staring at the wall made of skulls and bones.

"My goodness," he whispered to himself and patted the sweat from his forehead with his little green and gold handkerchief. "Things sure look different close up than they do from afar. Poor Nanny Reilly and Ned Franey. How terrified they must have been standing at the foot of a wall like this and then pounced on by those mean skeleguards. They surely are the two bravest children in Ireland."

King Brendan took a stake from the satchel over his shoulder and hammered it into the wall. He stood on it and bounced a little to test it for his weight.

"That does the trick," he said softly, so he hammered another one in about three inches above it. He continued that process for four stakes and then climbed them like it was a ladder. As he was starting his second series of steps for his ladder he heard the ferns rustle behind him. He didn't turn around, but continued to hammer in his stakes. He stepped up two more steps. He heard more rustling behind him, this time it was closer. Still he didn't turn around. He kept on going, one stake at a time, one step at a time. Tap, tap, tap, went his hammer. A moonlit shadow quickly moved across the wall to his right and disappeared. Immediately after that another shadow quickly moved across the wall to his left and disappeared. King Brendan saw the shadows but ignored them. He just kept tapping away as those shadows just became more and more plentiful and more and more frequent. Then, a cold chill went through him as one shadow approached him and darkened his entire surroundings. He looked over his right shoulder, and there was the Banshee staring him in the face. He, just like Nanny and Ned was terrified at the sight of her hook nose and pointed chin, warts around her face, no teeth, and black beady eyes.

"Ha, ha, ha," she laughed, "this is my best capture yet. Ha, ha, ha. Tonight, we all celebrate." She was elated.

The skeleguards were high-fiving each other and patting each other on the back. King Brian was such a trickster, he'd eluded her for centuries. Finally now he was in her grasp. He couldn't disappear like he normally did. His magic was no use to him now.

"I've been expecting you, King Brian, king of all the leprechauns of Coolrainy," said the Banshee calmly. "Welcome to the Banshee's Cradle for the last time. Your carriage awaits you. Please allow my skeleguards to escort you to your accommodations for the evening, ha, ha, ha."

King Brendan, who the Banshee thought was King Brian, looked beyond the Banshee and saw an army of skeleguards in their tattered uniforms lined up to take him into the Cradle. He noticed one of the skeleguards was carrying a small wooden crate, just about the right size for him to stand in. The skeleguard placed it on the ground and opened the door of the crate wide. Then he gestured to King Brendan with his bony forefinger to come down his ladder and step inside.

"My dear Banshee," answered King Brendan with a smile as he removed the satchel with the wooden stakes from his shoulder and hung them on the top step with his hammer. "Surely you can provide better accommodations than that for your royal guest. After all, you appear to be happy to see me, why not show it?" He then proceeded to step backwards down the ladder.

"I intend to, Mr. Leprechaun King," replied the Banshee with a similar smile. "You've known me long enough by now to give me more credit than that. I always take special care of my VIP guests. In fact, I even have your cloak all laid out for you. I thought you might like that."

"Oh yes, I'd love that," said King Brendan. "How did you know I like to wear my cloak for Santa on Christmas Eve? Sure, won't I be having a nice cup of hot tea with him later as I pass on the leprechaun's letters?"

The Banshee's smile left her face, her eyes and lips tightened and her tone changed back to her usual wicked raspy voice. She didn't like King Brendan's calm, confident demeanor. The Banshee began to question herself. Maybe he knew something she didn't? This particular leprechaun King is the smartest of the lot. Maybe he and Mr. Santa Claus are in cahoots? That dreaded Santa Claus spoke to her in the same manner.

Once again the Banshee became doubtful of her plans. What seemed foolproof to her may not be foolproof to this silly leprechaun king. He must have something up his sleeve. That's how he is, crafty and slithery, he has always been like that, why would he be any different now?

"You silly little man," she snapped. "If you're planning something, remember I have those two whiny children and that ridiculous dog at my mercy, and if you think I'm going to put you all in the same cell to buddy up, you are mistaken. You're going under lock and key under my nose."

"Take me wherever you will, Banshee," he replied calmly, "but mark my words, nothing you do is going to change the outcome. Tonight, I'll be having a hot cup of tea with Santa Claus. I'll be giving the leprechaun's letters to him, and, I'll be pointing out the best behaved leprechauns who deserve a little something extra this Christmas."

Anger came very easy to the Banshee. She at this moment was ready to explode. King Brendan had frustrated her more than she could tolerate. She was tight-lipped and rigid.

She inhaled in anger, and turned to the skeleguard who had King Brendan's cage. "Take him to my quarters, and don't let him out of your sight." She had nothing more to say to King Brendan. The Banshee abruptly turned and took long quick strides back into the Cradle. Anger radiated from her. The ferns in her path wilted and died one by one as she passed them.

King Brendan stepped into his new accommodations with a smile on his face. He was genuinely scared, but it was imperative that he didn't show it. The Banshee thrived on the fear others had for her. It made her laugh and feel powerful. King Brendan knew tonight above all nights, he had to show why he was a king. He had to be courageous.

CHAPTER SEVENTEEN

King Brian, King Cormac, King Rory and Princess Tara were watching the whole show from a safe distance behind the ferns and tall grass.

"Uncle Brian, do you think we have made the Banshee too mad?" asked Princess Tara in a soft voice, as she was now concerned for her fellow Rescueteers.

"Not at all, my little princess," whispered King Brian, putting his arm around his niece to reassure her. "The Banshee was born angry, we've just added a little necessary fuel to the fire, that's all. Don't you worry about a thing." King Brian removed his little green and gold handkerchief from his trouser pocket and wiped his brow and the back of his neck with it. Even though things were going according to plan, he too was concerned, as the Banshee was also quite clever.

He looked at King Rory. King Rory acknowledged his look with a nod, "It's time for Tara and I to make tracks," said King Rory quietly. "Are you ready Tara?"

Princess Tara stood tall, pulled her riding boots up by the boot straps, brushed herself off and tugged on the lapels of her riding jacket. "I'm good and ready, my dear father," she said as she tossed her long red ponytail over her shoulder. "Lead the way."

Nanny and Ned stood before Santa Claus not knowing what to say. They spent the last two weeks talking about Santa and their letters to him, and now they were speechless. Santa had many children stand before him in awe over the years so he recognized these symptoms very well. He placed both hands on his knees and hunched down to Nanny and Ned's level. He looked over the rim of his glasses.

"Well," he said with a broad smile, "who do we have here?"

Ned looked at Nanny indicating that she tell Santa who she is first.

Nanny blurted out, "Nanny Reilly," and then nudged Ned.

"I'm Ned Franey," answered Ned just as quickly as Nanny did.

"And you are?" Santa looked directly at Henry Daly who was sitting to attention beside Nanny waiting for his turn.

"Henry Daly," said Henry with a smile as broad as Santa's.

"Ho, ho, ho," laughed Santa. "I see you've been given the gift of speech, Henry Daly."

"Oh I forgot," said Henry, putting his paw up to his mouth to stop the words. "It's a secret. I'm not supposed to talk in here. If the Banshee hears me she will keep me for herself." Henry kept his paw to his mouth. "Shh."

"Ho, ho, ho," laughed Santa again. He stood up straight. "Don't you worry, Henry Daly. I keep a lot of secrets, and I promise you I'll keep yours." Santa reached into his leather pouch on his belt and took out his little black book. "I know those names. Let me see here." He put his glasses on the bridge of his nose, licked his middle finger and began flicking and glancing through the pages mumbling Nanny Reilly, Ned Franey and Henry Daly.

Nanny and Ned thought Santa could have read their letters, and torn them up, how else could Santa have their names in his little black book?

"Here we are," said Santa. "I have the three of you down under 'exceptional children and dog'. My scouting elves told me, and they're never, ever wrong."

"We're down under 'exceptional?'" said Nanny.

"Are you sure it's us?" added Ned. This was a new adjective for Ned to absorb, 'exceptional'. He had been referred to as many adjective's in his young life to denote his qualities, but certainly not exceptional.

"Yes I'm absolutely sure it's you," smiled Santa. He again bent down to their level and held his little notebook in front of them. "Look," he said, "read for yourselves."

Nanny and Ned peered into the little book. Ned put his finger under each letter of his name and spelled it out. "N-e-d F-r-a-n-e-y.

That's just how I spell my name," said Ned in disbelief as he looked at Nanny.

"And there's my name," pointed out Nanny, N-a-n-n-y Reilly, and Henry Daly's name. Exceptional," she read, as she pointed out the heading on top of the page to Ned. Henry Daly couldn't read, but he still got up on his back legs and peered into the notebook to see what Nanny and Ned were reading.

"Ho, ho, ho," laughed Santa, he was enjoying his young company very much, almost to the point he forgot where he was.

"Why are we exceptional?" asked Nanny, she was just as bewildered as Ned. She had been called mischievous, forgetful, good by her parents, her teacher and King Brian, that was the closest she ever got to exceptional.

"Yeah," added Ned, "where were we when we became exceptional?" Ned's mind wandered back his bully days and the amount of times he stood in the corner with his face to the wall.

"My elves are everywhere the children are," replied Santa. "Whether it's school," he paused and looked at Ned over the rim of his glasses.

Ned swallowed.

"In the playground, at home," said Santa looking at Nanny.

I knew it, thought Nanny. He knows I whine about my hair.

"Or out playing in the fields," continued Santa. "Let me see, on a summer's eve I have written here in my book. I don't have where you were, but I do have exceptional behavior for helping mankind."

"We were here," answered Nanny.

"Yeah, we were here," Ned quickly responded.

"That's true," added Henry Daly, backing Nanny and Ned up.

"You were here," said Santa, now it was his turn to be in a state of shock. "Here in the Banshee's Cradle?"

"Yes, here in the Banshee's Cradle," said Nanny and Ned together. "We were skelecooks."

"And I was a skeledog," added Henry Daly with a big smile all around his snout.

Santa had to sit on the edge of the bed. "Some news is hard to absorb," he said as he looked directly at Ned. Ned understood and smiled back at Santa. Santa put his little black book back in his leather pouch, and retrieved his holly-printed handkerchief from his trouser pocket. He then opened the top button of his jacket and wiped his handkerchief all around his face and neck.

"We're the Rescueteers," said Nanny. "That's why we were here."

"We can normally snap our fingers, or we have our shillelaghs, but they are no good to us here this time," said Ned.

"The Banshee has a wish-blocking device all around the Cradle and the ferns and the grass died outside," continued Nanny.

"I'm to stay with Nanny and Ned, and I'm not supposed to be talking," said Henry Daly, as he sat smiling up at Santa.

"Slow down," said Santa as he held his palms up. "Take a deep breath and exhale."

Nanny, Ned, and Henry Daly inhaled and exhaled. They paused and waited for the okay from Santa to begin.

"Now," said Santa as he took a breath himself, "please tell me, why you were here before? What you did here? How did you get out? And what in heaven's name brought you back here. Nanny Reilly?" Santa pointed at Nanny. "Let's start with you." He nodded at Nanny, giving her the okay to start.

Nanny began what was the most eye-opening, intriguing story Santa had ever heard in all his years. How they became the Rescueteers and how they saved Fran O'Toole and Mike Donovan, two local fishermen from the Banshee. Now he knew why these two children, and Henry Daly were exceptional.

CHAPTER EIGHTEEN

King Rory led the way ducking behind tall grass and ferns. He too was headed for the east side wall of the Cradle where King Brendan was just captured. Princess Tara followed closely, holding on to the hem of his cloak for fear of separation. King Rory's crown was shifting as he ran and by the time they reached the east wall it was tilted over his eyebrows and he couldn't see above eye level. At the bottom of the wall he made sure Princess Tara was at his side.

"Stay stuck to me, Tara," he whispered. "Whatever happens, remember now, don't let anything intimidate you. Keep your composure at all times."

"Okay Father," replied Princess Tara as she stood staring at the skull and bones east wall and the climb they had before them.

King Rory straightened out his crown and followed Princess Tara's eyes. He too was wide-eyed as he stared at the ghastly skull and bone made wall.

"May all the Saints preserve us," he said. "How did we ever land ourselves in this Mess? That's the most daunting sight I have ever seen."

"It surely is, Father," answered Princess Tara. "Nanny and Ned must have been terrified."

"And your Uncle Brendan too," added King Rory. "Sure they all must have felt like we do now, scared out of our wits."

"Are you scared, Father?" asked Princess Tara.

"No, no, not at all Tara," quickly answered King Rory. "I'm over the shock of it now. It just looks worse than it is, so don't you be scared.

Soon all this will be over and we'll be enjoying a nice cup of hot tea with Santa Claus and all the Rescueteers later." He patted Princess Tara's back to reassure her. "All right then, let's get started." He rubbed his hands together, tossed his cloak over his shoulder and climbed the first step of King Brendan's ladder. As King Rory made his way up the ladder he avoided any eye contact with the skulls in the skull and bone wall.

Princess Tara had to let go her father's cloak to climb the ladder, but she kept as close as she could to him. She was no more than half a step behind him until they got to the last step King Brendan put in.

"We have to continue with the steps from here, Tara," said King Rory. "Hold on tight until I get the first of these stakes in." King Rory reached for the hammer and the satchel of stakes left behind by King Brendan and began tapping away. Tap, tap, tap went the hammer again; step by step again the ladder grew.

Princess Tara hung on tight. She looked over her right shoulder to see if any predators were lurking in the moonlit forest. She thought she heard something coming from the left so she quickly turned her head to look over her left shoulder. There was nothing there. As King Rory kept tapping away one stake at a time, Princess Tara kept looking back and forth and all around her, she had no peace just one restless moment after the other.

King Rory reached the top of the wall and then he began the descent with the stakes at the other side. Princess Tara was now sitting on top of the wall and looking down into the Banshee's Cradle. There were old dead pine trees everywhere. Some still rooted and some lying spread out on the ground with broken limbs and uprooted trunks. It looked like a pine tree graveyard to her. How sad that happened to the beautiful, tall, majestic pine trees.

"Father," whispered Princess Tara, "will we ever be able to use our leprechaun magic here at the Banshee's Cradle and make things alive and green again?"

King Rory didn't look up, his brow was beaded up with sweat as he continued to tap away. "I'm not sure Tara," he answered. "The Banshee has our magic blocked out pretty good. It seems to me if we tried any magic, more things would die."

Princess Tara had no response. She knew her father was right. After all, her Uncle Brian proved that when the ferns died as he attempted to bring Santa back outside the Cradle.

"Come step down now Tara, and stay close," said King Rory. Princess Tara slowly and carefully began her descent. Once again she watched from all angles to see if anything was lurking in the shadows of the night. One moment she thought she heard something over there, the next moment she thought she heard something over here. Her ponytail was busy swinging back and forth and her restless moments continued.

"One last stake and we're there," King Rory was happy to say. Even though it was a chilly night he was quite warm and feeling a little tired after his arduous task. "I'm glad that's over with," he said with a sigh of relief. "I surely thought my hammer tapping days were over the moment I put this crown on." He placed the hammer in the satchel and placed it on the ground. He then stretched out his hand to help Princess Tara off the last step.

"Allow me," interrupted a wicked raspy voice.

King Rory stepped back in fright as the Banshee towered over him. She had her army of skeleguards behind her.

"Father, Father," cried Princess Tara. She was hanging on for dear life to a step and turning her body into the wall to avoid the grasp of the Banshee. "Don't let her get me—please don't let her get me."

King Rory plunged forward to grab Princess Tara from the ladder, but the Banshee intervened. She picked King Rory up by the scruff of the neck with one of her long fingernails and picked Princess Tara up by the scruff with another fingernail. She held them both as high in the air as she could looking from one to the other and laughing wickedly.

"Ha, ha, ha, I knew it, I knew it, I knew it," she laughed. "I knew that stupid leprechaun King Brian had something up his sleeve. I knew the invasion into my Cradle didn't stop with him."

King Rory and Princess Tara were kicking out their feet and swinging their arms in the air trying to free themselves from the Banshee's grip, but to no avail. King Rory tired fast, he was already worn out from working the hammer, but Princess Tara refused to stop fighting. She kicked and punched as hard and as fast as she could.

"Let me go, let me go," she yelled.

"Aren't you a lively one?" the Banshee said to Princes Tara. "Maybe I'll find some high energy work in the Cradle for you, ha, ha, ha."

"Please Banshee," pleaded King Rory, his face drawn and tired looking, "she is only a child. Let her go and take me with you."

"You're as stupid as that silly brother of yours," laughed the Banshee. "He made me so angry with his calm demeanor and his cocky smile, he made me think he was up to something, Then it dawned on me. He left the hammer and those wooden stakes on the east wall for you. Who else would be small enough to climb that ladder? This little thing here," she held Princess Tara close to her face, "was a bonus."

The Princess took advantage of being that close to the Banshee's nose. She took aim and punched the Banshee as hard as she could. The Banshee laughed and laughed at Princess Tara.

"That felt like you were swatting a fly from my nose," she laughed.

One of the skeleguards opened the door of a small crate, just like the one King Brendan was taken away in.

"I apologize for the tight accommodations," "she said smiling, "but I didn't expect my little leprechaun bonus." The Banshee put Princess Tara and King Rory on the ground. Immediately Princess Tara turned and ran as fast as she could.

"Run, Father, run," she cried as she headed toward the main entrance, but King Rory was too tired.

"It's no good, Tara, I'm finished," he said, his voice was tired, his body was tired, his shoulders were dropped and his head hung low. "I surrender." A skeleguard stopped Princess Tara in her tracks. He too picked her up by the scruff of the neck. She began kicking and punching out again.

"Let me go, let me go," she continued to yell. By now the whole army of skeleguards, together with the Banshee were laughing hard at Princess Tara. She and King Rory were ushered into their tiny cage and the door slammed behind them.

"Take them to my quarters to join that other silly leprechaun king," said the Banshee, "but wait until I get there. I want to see his face."

Princess Tara cried bitter tears. King Rory held her in his arms. They were both headed to the unknown and, they were both gripped with fear.

CHAPTER NINETEEN

Nanny, Ned, and Henry Daly had just finished their story when the laughs of the Banshee rang out throughout the Cradle. Santa placed his hands on his knees and stood up.

"It sounds to me like the Banshee has another captor or two," he said.

The thick wooden door at the top of the stairwell swung open and the Banshee came down the steps in a hurry, Her long gown dragged over each step and clouds of dust followed her.

"I couldn't wait to tell you all the good news." Her smile was so wide her hook nose and chin literally touched. She swaggered to the cell door. "We have an extra guest who will soon be joining you all at departures. A little Princess she is.

"That's Princess Tara," said Nanny.

"I have the whole 'fan damily' in my quarters," jeered the Banshee. "The feisty little Princess, with Daddy Rory and Uncle Brian."

Santa appeared to be quite somber. "What's the matter, Mr. Santa Claus? You aren't so sure of yourself now. All your silly leprechaun friends have been captured.

Who's going to save you now?"

"You should let the children go, Banshee," replied Santa. "There's no need to put them through all this. I'm the one you want."

"Well, they're going to be here sooner or later, and I'd rather it be sooner," taunted the Banshee. "You will all walk the plank before sunrise. My skelattendants are getting departures ready right now. Oh how much fun we're going to have tonight." She abruptly turned and arrogantly strutted down the corridor.

King Brian and King Cormac took a deep breath. They felt enough time had passed after the capture of King Rory and Princess Tara. It was going to be daylight in a few hours and the clock was ticking. It was time for both of them to venture into the Cradle.

"I believe the Banshee's guard is down right now," said King Brian. "I hope everybody's all right." King Brian paused for thought. He was reflecting the capture of all his comrades. The last one he saw go over the wall was little Princess Tara, not the size of two cents and she was willing to punch out the whole brigade. King Rory and King Brendan, two of his three brothers. It seems his brothers only got into situations whenever they were involved with King Brian himself, otherwise they led a normal, quiet, uneventful leprechaun life. Nanny Reilly and Ned Franey, how brave those two children are, and how fast they were willing to help save Santa, they were troopers. Henry Daly, a dog with the heart of a lion. All the Rescueteers had one thing in common. They really cared.

"It's up to us now, Brother Cormac," said King Brian. "This entire mission is now in our hands. We can't fail."

"I know these are anxious moments in the Cradle for the Rescueteers," answered King Cormac. "Don't worry Brian, we won't fail."

King Brian and King Cormac crawled quietly and slowly toward the east wall of the Banshee's Cradle. They did their utmost to avoid disturbing any foliage whatsoever. If they heard a sound at all, they stopped cold, kept their heads down and waited for that sound to come and go. It was a long slow crawl to the Cradle. There were two skeleguards and two skeledogs at the main gate. The pair of kings watched them for several minutes. The skeleguards didn't seem to be too alert. They stood at ease and chatted back and forth to each other. The skeledogs lay quietly in front of the gate. Once in a while their ears would twitch as though they heard something, but then they would relax their ears again and sigh themselves into a state of quiet relaxation. It seemed to be a normal evening at the gate.

On went King Brian and King Cormac. Quietly shifting from elbow to elbow as their legs pushed them along. After ten minutes of turtle crawling they were yards from the east wall. They waited quietly in their crawl position, there was not a word between them. After several minutes when they felt they were safe, King Brian and King Cormac continued their crawl to the end of the east wall. Before they stood to make their move the brothers looked at each other and quietly gave each other a tight hand shake, then they calmly and methodically made their climb up King Brendan's ladder.

Meanwhile, in the Banshee's boudoir, King Brendan is propped up on a shelf above the Banshee's desk in his wooden cage. Princess Tara and King Rory are in a cage beside him. The Banshee is sitting at her desk chuckling away to herself. She's writing a note on a piece of old rawhide, and using a finger bone as a pen, she dipped the fingernail in black ink, the note reads as follows,

> "To all the Banshees in Ireland. Hear ye, Hear ye,
> You are cordially invited to a departure celebration that none of us have ever known before. I have seven new arrivals, three of which, we have all been after since our time began, and four as a bonus. Soon they will all become my skeletees. I will then have the most elite staff of all times. I want you all to share in this moment with me as it will never happen again. As always, all departures are scheduled just before dawn. I have made special arrangements for your arrival and my skelechef is preparing a feast for all of us after the departure ceremony. There is no need to R.S.V.P. Just show up,
>
> Deceitfully Yours,
> The Banshee of Raven's Point

The Banshee stood from her chair and marched to her door. She opened the door wide and yelled down the dingy corridor, "skelesistant, skelesistant. Where are you? I need you here now."

Within seconds, the rattling of bones was heard in the distance from down the dismal corridor. The Banshee's skelassistant appeared in the dim light quite flustered. She had a thin scalp of long uncombed black hair. She wore a tattered and torn uniform similar to the skeleguards with one exception, hers had skelassistant poorly painted across the back. She held an old rag which served as a handkerchief to her forehead.

"You called for me Banshee, said the skelassistant as she continued to pat her forehead with the old rag. The skelassistant was nervous of the Banshee and it showed by her trembling bones and beads of sweat dripping from her forehead.

"I want one hundred of our fastest crows to get this message to all the Banshees as quickly as possible. They have to be here for this departure above all others. Call my skelechef, tell him to make a big batch of those lizard livers he made for the Banshee's Banquet last summer. Tell him we're having Banshees from all over Ireland again. Make sure the Banquet hall is ready, and make sure we have enough staff on duty. Go through the new arrivals list and see how many we can use as skeletrustees, and whatever you do, do not have any of my special seven do skeletrustee." The Banshee glared at her skelassistant. "They have all to stay under lock and key. I want to see the list of skeletrustees before they get their skeliforms, got that?"

"Yes, yes I do Banshee," answered the skelassistant as she began backing away from the Banshee. "I'm on it right away. The special seven stay in captivity, they won't be on the skeletrustee list. Don't you worry Banshee. I have everything under control."

"You better have," answered the Banshee, nothing must go wrong, everything must be perfect or you too will be back at the departure ceremony, not as a guest but as a captor.

The skelassistant quickly turned and rattled her way out the door of the Banshee's boudoir and down the dismal corridor. At the end of the corridor she turned to see if the Banshee was watching her, but not a sign of life anywhere. The skelassistant retrieved a nub of a candle from her raggedy trouser pocket and lit it from a bat torch overhead. She then continued down the corridor and around the corner. She quietly and carefully opened the rawhide and read the note the Banshee deemed so important.

"Three of which we have been after since time began," she read, she paused for thought, who could the three possibly be? The skelassistant rolled the rawhide back into a scroll and continued on her way to the dispatch crows.

CHAPTER TWENTY

King Brian and King Cormac quietly made their descent down King Brendan's ladder. When their feet touched the ground, they stood and stared at their surroundings. The Banshee's Cradle was most definitely the most fearsome intimidating place in the whole of Ireland. Even though King Brian had seen it before, it didn't soften the blow for him. Both he and King Cormac were stricken by the tall blackened pine trees with no needles, just bare limbs and dead ferns and foliage all around them. There were many fallen pine trees with broken dead limbs scattered all around them. It was a sure sign of despair and misery.

"I don't like this, Brian," whispered King Cormac. "This seems to be a place of no return."

"Not for us," answered King Brian quietly. "We have an invincible plan. So far everything is falling into place--we're so close to accomplishing our mission."

Suddenly overhead, a flock of the Banshee's crows with bugles strapped to their backs were flying off in different directions. They were cawing loudly, creating an uneasy feeling for King Brian and King Cormac.

"Get down," King Brian hissed in a loud whisper as several of the crows soared toward them. King Cormac kept his hands over his head as he lay face down amongst the dead and withered ferns. The crows flew on by without even a glance in their direction. They were on a specific mission for the Banshee.

"They must be messenger crows," whispered King Brian. "I'm willing to bet the Banshee is getting ready to gloat over her captures.

I'll be so bold as to say her guard is surely down now--she thinks she has all of us," chuckled King Brian, as he stood and brushed himself off. "But that does not mean we let our guard down."

"To be quite honest with you Brian," answered King Cormac, standing and looking at his surroundings, "I'm too scared to let my guard down. Just take a good look around. I'm expecting something to jump out as us any moment."

"Shh," whispered King Brian. He quickly threw himself to the ground again. King Cormac, without knowing why, also threw himself to the ground and buried his face. He was terrified. They could hear the rustling of dry foliage and an occasional snap of dry twigs. It was as though something was creeping up on them. King Cormac slightly lifted his head and glanced at King Brian. King Brian had his finger to his tightly sealed lips, indicating to Cormac not to say a word. They both lay in complete silence for several minutes. The rustling noises got closer. Dark shadows slowly crept up on them. Beads of sweat appeared on both kings foreheads. Fear had taken over. They lifted their heads and standing over them were two skeleguards. King Brian and King Cormac gave each other a solemn look. They were both thinking the same thing. This wasn't supposed to happen. A cold shiver went down their spines. What about Nanny Reilly, Ned Franey and Henry Daly? What about Princess Tara, King Rory, King Brendan, and Santa Claus? Now who was going to save them?

CHAPTER TWENTY-ONE

Santa was devastated to hear the Banshee had King Brian, King Rory and Princess Tara upstairs in her boudoir. He sat at the edge of the bed with his face buried in the palms of his hands, sobbing his heart out.

"If I hadn't of been so gullible when the Banshee approached me. None of us would be in this mess. I'm to blame for all of this. I've broken my own cardinal rule and let the children down. Shame on me."

"Don't cry, Santa," said Nanny. It was very difficult for Nanny and Ned to see Santa cry. Nanny put her arms around him, "The Banshee doesn't have King Brian in her boudoir—she only thinks she does."

"Yeah," said Ned with a big smile across his freckled face, "the Banshee has King Brian's twin brother King Brendan."

"That's right," added Nanny. "King Brian and King Cormac are going to rescue all of us tonight."

"And I'm going to make sure you all get out ahead of me," continued Henry Daly. "I'm the anchor dog," He smiled with his familiar broad smile showing all his teeth.

"Our plan is invincible," said Nanny as her face lit up and she smiled a bright smile at Santa.

"King Brian said the Banshee won't know what hit her," said Ned still wearing his freckled face smile.

"Wait a minute, wait a minute," said Santa, he raised his hands in the air to slow his young visitors down. He shook his head and rubbed his forehead. "You three are just full of surprises. Now, let's do this again." He stood from the cell bed and gestured to Nanny, Ned, and Henry Daly to have a seat. "I'm going to sit here on the floor against the wall in case I faint with shock, at least I won't have far to fall." Santa sat against the cell wall. He braced his body and his mind for what he was about to hear. "Okay Nanny Reilly, let's start with you again. Take another deep breath and start from the beginning." Santa looked at Nanny over the rim of his half glasses and nodded for Nanny to start what was going to be as fascinating as the last story Nanny began.

Nanny took a deep breath. "We had a meeting of the Rescueteers around a big mushroom at Magandy's Pond on how to rescue you from the Banshee's Cradle," she said.

"Magandy's Pond is now our official headquarters," added Ned with a big smile, in case Nanny forgot to mention it. "We're the Rescueteers and we go on rescue missions," he said proudly. "So we have to have a headquarters to do our strategic planning."

Santa's body shifted a little. "You have headquarters?" he asked.

"We have to," said Nanny, "because we have a lot of secret things to discuss."

"And we have a round mushroom just like the Knights of the Round Table," continued Ned.

"I sniff the air around us to make sure nobody is sneaking up on us and listening to our plans," said Henry Daly.

"Of course," Santa replied in his deep soft voice. He too took a deep breath and resolved to listen with open ears and without question, to Nanny, Ned, and Henry Daly. "Please continue, Nanny Reilly," he added.

"Myself, Ned and Henry Daly were at the round mushroom with King Brian and his twin brother King Brendan," said Nanny

"King Rory and his twin brother King Cormac were there too," said Ned

"And so was Princess Tara," smiled Henry Daly.

"King Rory, King Brendan and King Cormac came in white tornados," continued Nanny. King Brendan looks exactly like King Brian and King Cormac looks exactly like King Rory."

Santa nodded continuously, trying to absorb what his young company was telling him. He had made up his mind to let them tell their story their way. If he listened intently, he would get the general gist of it.

"And then Princess Tara punched her way out of King Rory's tornado," said Henry Daly. "I thought she was a predator and I was ready to pounce on her."

"She didn't want to miss anything and was ready for action," added Ned.

"King Brian asked King Rory, King Brendan, King Cormac and Princess Tara to solemnly swear to watch out for all Rescueteers. Then he touched them on the shoulders with his shillelagh and by the power vested in King Brian, there were officially sworn in as Rescueteers," said Nanny

"And King Brendan snapped his fingers and made the big round flat-topped spotted mushroom appear," continued Ned.

"We sat around the mushroom and made our invincible plan to rescue you," smiled Henry Daly again.

"I see," said Santa. "And what was the plan?" he reluctantly asked.

"We had to put our checklist together and then Ned, Henry Daly and myself were to be caught first by the Banshee," continued Nanny.

"We rehearsed how we were going to sneak up on the Banshee's Cradle and how she was going to think King Brian was in Nanny's backpack," said Ned.

"And I was to growl, but not bite her," said Henry Daly. "If I bit her she would separate me from Nanny and Ned. If I didn't growl, King Brian said she would suspect we were up to no good."

"King Brian is very clever," said Santa, as he patted his brow with his holly printed handkerchief. This story was taking its toll on him. Even though he was aware of all the leprechauns and the Banshee, he would never tie them all in together. He had never in all his years around children ever heard something so incredible.

Nanny, Ned, and Henry Daly told the whole story from start to finish to Santa. They explained in their own words how Nanny and King Brendan had a checklist, and how significant the items were. King Brendan's checklist was the satchel of wooden stakes and his hammer, allowing him to pave the way for King Rory and Princess Tara, and finally for King Brian and King Cormac. Nanny's checklist was the twenty-foot nylon rope and a flash light. So it would appear that they were trying to sneak over the Cradle wall. The magic chocolate bars because the Banshee has a weakness for chocolate. She has no teeth and couldn't chew anything, but the chocolate she didn't have to chew, it would melt in her mouth. It was important that the Banshee absorbed the magic chocolate and then fall asleep. A sewing needle and a spool of black thread to sew the Banshee to her bed after she fell asleep, just in case she woke up too early. The tin whistle in the key of 'd' was King Brian's grand finale idea.

They told Santa how the Banshee would think she had King Brian when she captured King Brendan. How King Brendan kept the Banshee's suspicions aroused by being so nonchalant about being captured. And finally when the Banshee caught King Rory and Princess Tara, how her guard would be down thinking she has all the Rescueteers. Then King Brian and King Cormac could sneak into the Cradle using King Brendan's ladder without being noticed and rescue everybody after the Banshee ate her chocolate and fell asleep.

After hearing the whole rescue mission plan, Santa sighed a big sigh. He understood the plan well now. It was based on decoys and distractions, like any good rescue mission should be.

"I thank you all from the bottom of my heart," said Santa with a warm smile. He was humbled by the children's fearless efforts to save him. "I compliment you on your bravery. You truly are the two bravest children in Ireland, and the bravest dog." He patted Henry Daly on the head to emphasize his appreciation.

Nanny, Ned, and Henry Daly blushed at Santa acknowledging their bravery. Nanny and Ned thought back to their initial moments of fear. How it took a lot of strutting and hat tipping around Nanny's bedroom to build up enough courage to even get started on their mission.

"You have put my mind at ease. It seems like all we do now is wait for King Brian and King Cormac, and that should be in the next couple of hours as the early hours of Christmas Eve is upon us," continued Santa. "Won't the Banshee be surprised to wake up and find us all gone. Ho, ho, ho."

Nanny, Ned, and Henry Daly joined Santa in his laughter. They had no idea both King Brian and King Cormac were discovered by two skeleguards.

CHAPTER TWENTY-TWO

After the Banshee rudely dismissed her skelassistant, she returned to her boudoir.

"This is definitely the most prestigious night of my whole career," she said. "I will surely have celebrity status in the world of Banshees. I can't wait to see the reaction of all my associates when they see my array of new arrivals. They're going to think I'm the best Banshee to come down the turnpike." She looked at her portrait above her bed. "I may have a new one of those done. I've graduated from being the best to being absolutely brilliant. I'm about to be put on a pedestal." The Banshee was now feeling invincible, and swaggered over to her lineup of caged regal leprechauns: King Brendan, King Rory and Princess Tara.

"Merry Christmas to me," she sneered. "If I didn't know better, I'd say Santa came down my chimney and left you here for me to enjoy, ha, ha, ha. Not only did he leave you here, but I have all this chocolate to enjoy. I never knew Christmas was as much fun as this."

"You're a mean old witch," cried Princess Tara as she shook the bars of her tiny cage. "Let us out of here."

"Are you totally stupid?" replied the Banshee. "Why would I let you out of there? You're my claim to fame, soon all the Banshees in Ireland will be here to witness the three of you and your foolish counterparts with Mr. Santa Claus become my skeletees." She picked up the cage Princess Tara occupied with her father King Rory and peered into it. Her long hook nose touched the bars. "Soon you won't even know your own name and where you came from. Your brain will be mine. And you will do everything I say, just like all the other skeletees here. No one has a name and no one has a brain, what do you think of that?"

"This is what I think," replied Princess Tara, she reached out through the bars of her cage, grabbed the Banshee's nose and twisted it as hard as she could.

All the Banshee could do was laugh at Princess Tara. She pulled her head back and placed Princess Tara back on her shelf. "Ha, ha, ha, maybe I should keep you as you are, I find you to be quite amusing," she laughed.

"I'm going to get out of here," replied Princess Tara. "And you're going to be sorry you ever laid eyes on me."

"Ha, ha, ha," the Banshee continued to laugh heartily. In jest, she made her body tremble. "I'm shaking in my shoes—please don't hurt me."

Princess Tara plonked herself down on the floor of her cage. She folded her arms tightly and pouted. She was silently waiting for the moment the Banshee would fall asleep and Uncle Brian and Uncle Cormac would show up to rescue them. Then the shoe will be on the other foot and the Banshee will be truly sorry.

"As for you, King Brian of Coolrainy," the Banshee glared at King Brendan, "you have been a thorn in my side since time began. You're going to be the first departure on my list. Then I'll parade you around departures. I want all your comrades to see the mighty King Brian with no name and no brain. You're going to be my personal skelechaun, ha, ha, ha."

King Brendan glared back at the Banshee through the bars of his cage. He had to be careful in his answer and not to appear too cocky and make the Banshee suspicious of anything. "Well then Banshee, you better make sure you do a good job when you send me to departures, because once a leprechaun always a leprechaun." King Brendan smiled and put his face against the bars. "Have you ever known a leprechaun without a trick up his sleeve?"

The Banshee paused for thought. What that silly leprechaun King was saying could be true. The words Santa Claus had said to her earlier rang in her ears. "You underestimate the powers of the universe." She abruptly turned in anger and went directly to her loose floorboards and stomped her foot down hard on them. The boards popped up and once again the Banshee retrieved several rawhides.

King Brendan, King Rory and Princess Tara alerted themselves to this. They watched in eager silence as the Banshee went through each rawhide and then went through her development plans for the Banshee's Cradle.

"Coolrainy," she mumbled, "Ballineskar, mmm, Ballyvaloo, Ballyconniger." Her three captors were straining their ears to pick up any words that they may recognize. They heard the Banshee name all their villages, "All mine," she said. "Secret tunnel, wish-blocking device on."

What could the Banshee be plotting? There's more to this than meets the eye. The Banshee halfway convinced herself everything was set in concrete and nothing could possibly go wrong. She exhaled and rolled up the rawhides again and placed them back under the floorboards. But there was one more thing to check. Without looking at her curious audience she then marched to her closet and with one swoop, separated her untidy attire. King Brendan, King Rory and Princess Tara were now on their toes and straining to see what moves the Banshee was making. She fumbled with the red brick hiding her bunch of keys. She pulled out the brick and retrieved her keys. With her long narrow bony fingers she chose a particular key, hurried to her door, flung it open and disappeared in a cloud of dust.

"I'm worried," was King Rory's response to what he had just witnessed. "The Banshee is plotting something major. Did you hear her say Coolrainy, Ballineskar, Ballyvaloo, Ballyconniger all mine. What's that about?"

"It sounds like the Banshee is working on taking over all our villages. I think she lured us here by kidnapping Santa," continued King Brendan. "She knew the Rescueteers were going to make attempts to save him, that's why she installed the wish blocking device. Once we crossed the line we were at the point of no return and she had us right where she wanted us, disarmed of our magic and disabled in these made to order cages."

"I believe you're absolutely right, Brother Brendan," answered King Rory. His body deflated and he sank down into his made to order cage.

"I heard her say secret tunnel and wish-blocking device on," said Princess Tara.

"In my mind, that means the wish-blocking device can be turned off. When Uncle Brian and Uncle Cormac get here and let us out, we should look for the secret tunnel."

"I'm sure Brian and Cormac are already in the Cradle. They're keeping a low profile until the Banshee eats the chocolate and falls asleep."

"I'm looking forward to that mean old Banshee being sewn to the bed," said Princess Tara with gritted teeth. "I wish she'd hurry on back here and eat that chocolate so we can get on with our rescue mission."

"Shh, be quiet," said King Rory. "Here she comes."

The Banshee was once again in good spirits. Obviously, her mind was put at ease. She sauntered into her boudoir and sighed. "My goodness," she said, "what an exhausting time of year Christmas can be. It surely does make you have all your I's dotted and T's crossed. After such an eventful few hours, I think I've earned myself a little treat." She went to her closet and replaced her bunch of keys behind the red brick, she then picked up Nanny's backpack. "Oh chocolate bars, oh chocolate bars," she sang like the Christmas tune, 'Oh Christmas tree, oh Christmas tree.' King Rory, King Brendan and Princess Tara glanced at each other. This was the moment they had been waiting for. King Rory looked at Princess Tara and held his finger to his lips, indicating to her not to say a word that would stop the Banshee in her tracks. He knew his daughter could be a little feisty and outspoken, but this time she needed to be absolutely quiet. Princess Tara understood her father's gesture, tightened her lips and nodded.

"Ah, two bars of melt in my mouth milk chocolate, and two bars of melt in my mouth dark chocolate," sighed the Banshee as she upturned Nanny's backpack and the contents fell out. She picked up the needle and thread. "What would a silly child do with a sewing needle and thread?" She shook her head and tossed them on the floor with the rest of her mess. "And look at this," she said. She held up the tin whistle and threw it like a boomerang across the room. "There'll be no music of any kind in the Banshee's Cradle. I hate music."

These were anxious moments for King Rory, King Brendan and Princess Tara. They watched the Banshee toss the wrappers on the floor and gorge on the chocolate as if she hadn't eaten in days. She kept piling it in. Milk chocolate, then dark chocolate, square after square.

"Mmm, mmm, mmm," was all she could say. Her mouth was too full to talk. Her chin and nose moved in unison as she moved the melting chocolate around in her mouth. As soon as she had room in her mouth for more chocolate she piled it in. This ritual continued until all the chocolate was gone.

"Ah, that was just what the doctor ordered," she said with a sigh of relief and repeatedly smacking her lips together. "I think I'll take a quick forty winks before the festivities begin." She yawned and stretched her arms up and out as long as she could. Then she lay on her unmade bed and directed her weary eyes toward her captors. "Wake me in an hour," she said smiling and showing the residue of melted chocolate all around her toothless gums. "We can't be late." Her eyes closed and her body relaxed. For several minutes, the Banshee's boudoir was totally silent. Then like a jolt in the atmosphere, loud and heavy snoring filled the air. The Banshee was out for the count.

"Finally," exhaled Princess Tara. "I thought she'd never pass out." King Rory and King Brendan both rubbed their hands together in excitement and wiggled their bodies. The exhilaration was overwhelming.

"Brian and Cormac should be here any minute," chuckled King Brendan. "What a great plan we came up with. All we have to do now is wait."

They waited patiently and kept their eyes on the door expecting it to open and for King Brian and King Cormac to walk in and grace them with their presence. Half an hour went by and the door never opened.

CHAPTER TWENTY-THREE

The two skeleguards escorted King Brian and King Cormac to the rear of Dreary Castle. Not a word was said by either skeleguard as they directed the two leprechaun kings through what seemed to be a hidden pathway. The leading skeleguard moved dead ferns and weeds out of the way as King Brian and King Cormac followed. The second skeleguard replaced the foliage after everyone got through.

"Why are they covering our tracks and why are we going to the rear of the castle?' whispered King Cormac.

"They're being very careful about something," answered King Brian quietly.

The leading skeleguard stopped and turned around. He bent his skeletal frame down as low as he could and faced King Brian. He put his bony forefinger to his mouth and quietly said, "Shh."

King Brian quietly acknowledged the skeleguards request, remembering it was just ten minutes ago himself and King Cormac were in the same mode of complete and utter silence as they made their way to the Banshee's Cradle.

When they got to the base of the castle wall the skeleguards carefully looked around them. Then the lead skeleguard reached into a pile of dead ferns and opened a trap door in the ground. The ferns on the trap door stayed intact. They appeared to be purposely well tied on. The leading skeleguard then picked up King Brian's ten-inch frame, carried him down a dark stairway and placed him on the sandy floor of a candlelit tunnel. The second skeleguard handed King Cormac to the leading skeleguard as he pulled the trap door closed over his head.

Quickly and quietly the group moved their way through a winding tunnel. As they got closer to the end of the tunnel it got brighter. And then, as though the heavens opened they came upon a brightly lit cave. The Banshee's skelassistant sat on a well-crafted high back chair at a nicely made round wooden table. Underneath the table was a perfectly woven rug. This was a far cry from what King Brian had seen during his last visit to the Banshee's Cradle.

"Please come in and join us," said the lead skeleguard in a calm, well-spoken voice. "I apologize for not speaking outside. I didn't want to be overheard."

"We do know why you're here," said the second skeleguard, as he moved quickly and bent down to pick up King Brian. The lead skeleguard reached for King Cormac. They sat both kings on two impressive hand sewn green silk cushions fit for a pair of kings in the middle of their table.

"You know why we're here?" responded King Cormac with raised eyebrows and at the same time he and King Brian were admiring the beautifully hand crafted cushions. "And why might we be here?"

"We know you're here to rescue Santa Claus and your associates," said the skeleguard.

King Brian and King Cormac had no response. They weren't sure whether to agree or disagree. They instinctively let the skeleguard continue.

"And we also know that time is of the essence. The departure ceremony will begin before daybreak, that's in about one hour. The Banshees from all over Ireland will start arriving shortly, so I'll be brief and to the point."

"Please do," King Brian politely replied. He was in no position to question or interrupt this commanding skeleguard. The skeleguard was absolutely right, time was of the essence. The skeleguard turned his skeletal frame and looked around at his comrades, he then turned his attention back to the two leprechaun kings perched on the cushions in the center of their table.

"We are the underworld of the Banshee's Cradle and we want to help you," the skeleguard bowed his head slightly. "We're at your disposal."

The skelassistant nodded in agreement. She smiled a broad smile at the pair of kings while displaying a very full mouthful of teeth with no gums.

King Brian and King Cormac were taken aback--not only by the skelassistant's unflattering smile, but also by this unexpected occurrence. The last thing they expected from any of the skeleguards or skeletees was help.

"The underworld," both kings said together. To the kings that meant a rebellion brewing. Were they going to be hauled into something against their will for the sake of the cause?

"And you want to help us," continued King Brian.

"Yes and yes," promptly answered the skeleguard. "Allow me to quickly brief you on our position here in the Cradle. The skeleguard sat in his nice cushioned chair. "As you know, the Banshee captures whoever she can and turns them into her skeletees by way of departures. Once anyone has gone through departures, they're owned and operated by the Banshee. In other words, as the Banshee puts it herself, "No name and no brain."

"Saints preserve us," replied King Cormac, his thoughts immediately went to the other Rescueteers. "Then what happens to the skeletee?"

"Unfortunately," replied the skelassistant, "the skeletee thinks that is it. That is who they are from here on in and they accept it. They have no memory of their past, what their name was, or where they came from, and they don't seem to care."

"Each skeletee is processed, given a skeliform and put in whatever department they're needed most."

"Why are you three here so different?" asked King Brian as he admired the craftsmanship of the table and chairs and also the magnificent hand sewn cushions both he and King Cormac sat on.

"Because we have found a way to break away from the ……" the skeleguard raised his bony fingers to signal inverted commas. "run of the mill skeletee," he smiled.

"And how have you managed to do that?" quizzed King Cormac.

"Isn't it obvious?" said the skelassistant. "Everyone that comes in here has meat on their bones and they're scared. After they go through departures, they become a skeletal frame with no brain. Therefore, we know we came in with meat on our bones and we were scared."

"What the skelassistant is saying is," interrupted the skeleguard, "we want to get back to the way we were before the Banshee captured us. We know there's another world out there, it's still inside of us." He stood and held up the hand crafted cushion he was sitting on as proof of something more than being the Banshee's skeletee. He stood behind his high-backed chair and held both sides of it with his skelehands. "We have a talent, a gift, a passion to share, a life in another world and we want to get back to it. If we help you, will you help us?"

King Brian and King Cormac were relieved they weren't being recruited unwillingly to the underworld. They could see what the skeleguard was saying was absolutely true. With accommodations like this inside the Cradle and such wonderfully crafted work they agreed wholeheartedly to help the skeleguards.

"Well, after hearing all that, and knowing we aren't going to start a rebellion," chuckled King Cormac. "I don't see why we all can't work together for the same cause. What do you think, Brian?"

"Absolutely," agreed King Brian. "you skeletees know your way around the Cradle a whole lot better than we do I'm happy to say."

"Well, that settles it then," said the lead skeleguard as he gave a gumless smile to his comrades. "Let's get the two of you back on your mission before it's too late.

CHAPTER TWENTY-FOUR

Ned and was sound asleep on the cell bed. He lay on his back with one leg on the bed and his other leg rested on the floor, his arms were above his head, his mouth was wide open and his cowboy hat was on his chest. Henry Daly lay on the cell floor beside Nanny with his head resting on his two front paws. Nanny and Santa sat on the cell floor with their backs against the wall.

"Ned and I were afraid to come here tonight," said Nanny as she looked at Ned and saw how peaceful and relaxed he was now. More relaxed than Nanny, she was far too anxious and couldn't fall asleep while waiting for King Brian and King Cormac. Ned must be in his Lone Ranger mode.

"I'd imagine so," replied Santa. "What kind of persuasion did it take to get you to come back here? I beg you to share it with me Nanny Reilly, as I'd like to be aware of such persuasion if I ever find myself having to return to the Banshee's Cradle."

"Boots and spurs on a wooden floor," answered Nanny with a frown. "That's what did it." If Ned hadn't of mentioned boots and spurs at Magandy's Pond, there was a good chance Nanny Reilly would never have gotten into the Annie Oakley mode and then convince Ned Franey he was the Lone Ranger.

"Boots and spurs on a wooden floor?" Quizzed Santa, he raised his eyebrows, turned his body toward Nanny and looked over his half rimmed glasses at her. "Please go on Nanny Reilly, this I must hear." Santa prepared himself to hear another outlandish story from Nanny. Even though he was in captivity in the worst possible place, under the worst possible circumstances, at the early hours of Christmas Eve, he was a tickled to have such wonderful company.

"While we were fishing at Magandy's Pond," began Nanny, "we were talking about what we were asking you for this Christmas. I told Ned I was asking for a cowgirl suit like Annie Oakley's, the kind with the fringes on it."

Santa nodded, "I know the very one," he said, "and I think it would suit you to a T."

"Then I said I'd be a real cowgirl with my hat, my pony and my cowgirl suit," continued Nanny.

"That's absolutely right," said Santa with a nod and a smile. "What more would a cowgirl need?"

"Boots and spurs," continued Nanny. "That's what Ned said he was asking you for because the Lone Ranger wears them and so does Annie Oakley. When Annie Oakley walks across a wooden floor you can hear the sound of her boots and the clank of her spurs, everybody knows who she is and they don't mess with her."

"That's very true," agreed Santa.

"Well," said Nanny, "we got our new recruits, we got our headquarters, we got out round table, we made our invincible plan to rescue you and I still felt afraid.

"Understandably so," said Santa. "I'd be afraid myself—what did you do then?"

"Henry Daly and I were sneaking out of bed," said Nanny. "I was fully dressed and ready to go, but I was still afraid. When I saw my sneakers on my feet I thought of boots and spurs instead. I put my cowboy hat on and I practiced walking like Annie Oakley across the room. I imagined I was wearing leather boots, clanking spurs and walking across a wooden floor. Nobody was going to mess with me. In my mind I was Annie Oakley, I felt brave and I was ready to get started on our mission."

"Very interesting," said Santa. "So you became your hero. And what about Ned?"

Nanny squirmed a little, this was the part that really did it. "Then I heard a knock on my window," continued Nanny. "It was Ned. He couldn't sleep because he was afraid too. So I told him I was Annie Oakley and going on the mission instead of Nanny Reilly. Ned really wanted to be brave and save you, but it wasn't easy. So I showed him how I got my courage and he could do the same and become the Lone Ranger. Then the Lone Ranger would go on the mission instead of Ned Franey. Ned liked that idea, so he practiced walking across the wooden floor, he imagined the sound of leather boots and clanking spurs. He imagined everybody tipping their hats at him because he just drove the bad guys out of town. After a little practice back and forth across my room, Ned believed he was the Lone Ranger. I felt twice as brave because there were two of us from the American Wild West and no one was going to mess with us."

Santa's smile never left his face. The imagination of a child is a glorious thing. That's really where the magic of Christmas comes alive, and that's what keeps him going year after year. "And who do you think you are now?" he asked.

"Nanny Reilly," said Nanny disappointedly. "I knew I wasn't really Annie Oakley, but it helped me to be brave just to pretend I was." She looked over at Ned as he continued to sleep away any woes he might have. Ned was certainly making the most of his heroic role.

"Well, Nanny Reilly," said Santa, "Annie Oakley was once a nine-and-three quarter-year-old girl too. I do believe she used to pretend she was Calamity Jane and she also asked me for a cowgirl suit with fringes."

"She did?" said Nanny. What great new this was for Nanny. "Imagine Annie Oakley asking you for the same cowgirl suit as me and to think she pretended to be Calamity Jane." Nanny gave a little chuckle, for now anyway, she felt just fine as herself. She relaxed against the cell wall and thought about Annie Oakley writing her letter to Santa. She wondered if Annie Oakley woke up with night knots in her hair every morning. Nanny was convinced she did. That's why she always wore her cowboy hat so nobody could see them.

Ned stretched and opened his eyes to see Nanny sitting on the floor beside Santa with her head resting against his arm, her cowboy hat was tilted to one side and she was sleeping peacefully. He sat up and put his hat on. The whole night came to his mind. Once again he was terrified.

"How are you doing Ned?" asked Santa.

"I'm fine," pouted Ned as he glared at Nanny. "How come Nanny wasn't wide awake and afraid?" he thought.

Santa could read Ned very well. He knew Ned was bothered by Nanny's display of peace and contentment, just as Nanny was bothered by Ned when he was quietly sleeping without a care in the world.

"Nanny looks quite at ease doesn't she?' said Santa.

"She certainly does," answered Ned still pouting.

"While you were peacefully sleeping," said Santa, "Nanny was telling me about her heroine Annie Oakley and your hero The Lone Ranger."

Ned sat up straight. He didn't realize he was peacefully sleeping, and he was hoping Nanny didn't tell Santa how much of a coward he was.

"Nanny talks too much," said Ned. "She and Henry Daly, they're always talking, talking, talking."

"I asked Nanny what kind of persuasion made you two come back in here as I would like to know," continued Santa. "After being in here once I'd have to dig very deep inside of me to find the courage to come back to the Banshee's Cradle a second time."

Ned was surprised to hear Santa say he would have to dig deep for courage, that's exactly what Ned and Nanny did.

"It wasn't easy," answered Ned as he remembered strutting across Nanny's bedroom and tipping his hat time and time again, imagining himself as the Lone Ranger about to save the day. "We did a lot of pretending and a lot more imagining until we saw ourselves braver than we were. Before we knew it we were giving away our prized possessions and playing over the moon and under the stars."

"I salute you both, Ned," smiled Santa. "I think you both found a secret to conquer many fears in your attempts to become brave."

"We did," said Ned.

"Absolutely," answered Santa with a chuckle. "You used your imagination in the right way. You thought how brave you were not how scared you were, and by persisting in your attempts you conquered your fear."

"We surely did, didn't we," smiled Ned. He thought how clever Nanny was to come up with the secret to conquer fear. He never would have thought she was that clever, in fact, he really thought she was quite the opposite. "It was Nanny's idea," continued Ned. "She was pretending and imagining first, then she showed me how to do it." Ned looked at Nanny again, this time through different eyes, he had newfound admiration for her. Maybe she wasn't that weird after all?

Santa laughed, "What a pair." He thought, for sure they were getting their boots and spurs this Christmas, and maybe even a red bandana.

CHAPTER TWENTY- FIVE

The snores of the Banshee continued without missing a beat. King Brendan, King Rory and Princess Tara were contemplating giving up on King Brian and King Cormac. They were no longer watching the door. They were now thinking the worst. They must have been caught. Maybe that's why the Banshee was so smug and relaxed when she came back from checking the secret tunnel. Otherwise King Brian and King Cormac would be here by now. Princess Tara was sitting on the cage floor with her knees pulled into her chest and her head resting on her knees. She was quietly sobbing. King Brendan and King Rory could hear Tara's quiet sobs. They wanted to tell her everything would be fine, but they too had a tremendous fear inside them and felt like crying too.

The door of the Banshee's boudoir quietly opened. Nobody paid any attention to it. Princess Tara felt a hand on her shoulder. She thought it was her father consoling her. "It's no use," she said, her head was still buried in her knees. They've been caught. We're all doomed."

"Well, I wouldn't say doomed lass. Isn't that a word that has point of no return attached to it?" said a familiar voice.

Princess Tara looked up. Her face lit up and she jumped to her feet. "Uncle Brian, Uncle Cormac, you're here, you're here," she cried. She jumped up and down with excitement. "Father, they're here. Uncle Brendan, they're here." Princess Tara was beside herself with joy.

"Saints preserve us, Brian," added King Brendan. "We were beginning to worry about the two of you. We thought sure the Banshee had you captured too."

"I wouldn't say we were beginning to worry, I'd say we were worried," said King Rory as he wiped the sweat from his brow with his shamrock printed handkerchief.

"We made a pit stop on our way," answered King Cormac, as he unlatched King Brendan's cage. "But it's too much to explain right now, we don't have the time."

As King Brian was opening Princess Tara's and King Rory's cage, Princess Tara was giving him the whole story of the red brick in the closet wall with a set of keys. "Then the Banshee stomped her foot on the floor and those floorboards right there popped up," she said pointing to the floorboards in particular.

"The Banshee has big plans for our villages," said King Rory. "We're all destined for doomsday if we don't stop her." King Rory jumped from the Banshee's desk and made his way to the loose floorboards to retrieve the rawhide scrolls.

King Brendan made his way to the Banshee's closet. "Brian and Cormac," he said, "help me up to that loose brick, let's find out what keys fit what door?"

King Brian and King Brendan quickly moved to the closet. They held hands and formed a step for King Brendan, but they were too short to reach the red brick.

"We need you to stand on my shoulder, Tara," said King Brendan. "Hopefully you'll be able to reach that loose brick."

Princess Tara quickly scrambled up all three of her uncles and stood on King Brendan's shoulders. "I can't reach it," she said gasping.

"Here take my shillelagh and try and reach it with that," said King Brendan as he handed Princess Tara his shillelagh.

King Brian and King Cormac were getting tired and sweating profusely.

"The two of you are beginning to get very heavy," said King Cormac. "Can you speed it up a little?"

Princess Tara was shaking in her attempts. Several times she almost fell. "I can't go any faster than I'm going. Keep still Uncle Cormac, you're making me shake and lose my balance." She used the closet wall to lean on as she slowly stood on her toes. She could now touch the brick with the shillelagh. She persistently prodded at the brick and it finally freed itself and fell to the ground. "Now I can't reach the keys," she gasped.

"Stand on my head," said King Brendan.

Princess Tara climbed to the next level, on top of her Uncle Brendan's head. She stepped inside his crown and stood on her toes, she stretched her arm with the shillelagh and barely touched the keys.

"I don't think I can hold on much longer," said King Brian. "My back is about to give in."

"I'm almost there, Uncle Brian," answered the little Princess. "Just bear with me for two more seconds. She persistently teased the keys with the shillelagh until they too fell to the floor. She then climbed down the tier of leprechauns and picked up the keys.

"I'm beat to pieces," said King Cormac as he slowly straightened himself up pressing his hands into his lower back.

"That's the most effort I've ever put into anything," said King Brian panting and wiping his brow with his handkerchief

"Our magic has spoiled us," added King Cormac, as he too huffed and puffed and stood upright.

King Brendan patted both his brothers on the back. "I like being spoiled," he smiled. "I think at this stage of the game, we're all too long in the tooth to have it any other way."

"Never mind your pains and aches," said King Rory, not paying too much attention to his brothers and their tired bodies. "Come and look at these plans." He had them spread out on the floor. "The Banshee has being doing her homework."

The four leprechaun Kings and the leprechaun Princess knelt on the floor and studied the scrolls.

"Look here," said King Rory. The Banshee has a secret tunnel going from underneath the Cradle, to the main entrance where there's a wish-blocking device switch installed. It releases a misty fog to absorb and disable the wish every time it's made. She then plans to continue with a tunnel from the main entrance on into Coolrainy. From Coolrainy, she's going to develop the tunnel and continue to Ballineskar, Ballyvaloo and stop at Ballyconniger." He pointed out the four villages. "At all these locations, she has plans to put wish-blocking devices and take all the residents including us."

"Well now," said King Brendan, "isn't it a fortunate occurrence for all of us that the Banshee kidnapped Santa Claus and we ended up here to discover her development plans? It's only a matter of time before she robs us of our leprechaun magic and our villages."

"We can find the wish-blocking device switch and turn it off," added Princess Tara.

"We're running out of time now," said King Cormac. "The first thing we need to do is rescue Nanny, Ned, Henry Daly and Santa.

"You're right," said King Brian. "Look—that's where they are." He pressed his forefinger onto the scroll. "X marks the spot and that's the door we go through" he pointed to the heavy oak door with blackened brass bolts inside the Banshee's boudoir. "Let's get them." He grabbed the dungeon scroll that marked the location of his young Rescueteers and abruptly stood.

"We'll take these scrolls with us too," said King Rory as he rolled them up and tucked them under his cloak.

"Look," said Princess Tara. "It's close to daybreak, the needle and thread is moving."

The sewing needle was in an upright position. The spool of thread spun itself in tight circles unraveling its thread. The thread then glided its way through the eye of the needle. The needle with its long string of thread rose in the air and hovered over the Banshee's bed. It then took a nose dive toward the Banshee. It swiftly and fluently began to sew the Banshee's gown in tight stitches to the bed.

"Ha ha," laughed King Brian as he rubbed his hands together and reiterated his request of the needle and thread,

"Before dawn awakes the land,
And the Banshee has the upper hand,
Rise and shine
Needle and thread,
Sew the Banshee
To her bed."

All five leprechauns with the Banshee's scrolls and her bunch of keys, carefully made their exit from the Banshee's boudoir through the heavy oak door and down the dark stairway, leaving the Banshee well tucked in and snoring away to her heart's content.

CHAPTER TWENTY- SIX

Nanny woke up to the chuckles of Santa. She was no longer scared. Her bravery issues seemed to have taken a back seat now that she knew she and Annie Oakley had similarities. Ned on the other hand was thinking how clever Nanny was and he smiled right at her as she woke. Henry Daly, even though he looked sound asleep beside Nanny, was wide awake and alert to all sounds around him. Henry quickly stood up and pricked his ears, he gave a short growl.

"What is it Henry Daly?" asked Santa. Henry heard activity from the top of the dark stairway and was looking in that direction. Santa peered over the rim of his glasses and there before his eyes appeared an array of leprechauns. Tears of joy rolled down Santa's rosy red cheeks.

"Bless you all," he said in low soft deep voice as the entourage of leprechauns approached him with smiling faces and a key to the cell door.

"King Brian," yelled Nanny as she jumped to her feet.

"We knew you would be here any minute," said Ned.

"And Princess Tara," continued Nanny, "you made it. I'm so happy to see everyone."

"Yeah," said Ned, "are we glad to see you."

Henry Daly couldn't contain himself. He ran as best he could in circles on the bed, he jumped off the bed and back on it again. He sat to attention wagging his tail. "It's great to see everybody," he said in his scratchy voice, with his familiar bright smile.

"It's great to see you too Nanny, Ned, Henry Daly and Santa," said Princess Tara as she ran into the cell to hug their legs. "It has been the longest 5 hours of my life."

"And the longest 24 hours of my life, ho, ho, ho," laughed Santa. "Although my last few hours has been very entertaining." He turned to Nanny and Ned and looked at them over the rim of his glasses. "But I am ready to go back to the North Pole and get Christmas Eve underway."

"I'm afraid we can't go back just yet," said King Brian. "Another issue has arisen here in the Cradle that we have to tend to before we leave. If not, our rescue mission here is all in vain."

"In vain?" quizzed Santa with raised eyebrows.

"I'm afraid so," said King Brendan. King Cormac and King Rory nodded in agreement with their brothers.

"The Banshee has plans to take over all our villages and its occupants," continued King Brian. "If we leave now, the chances of us getting back in here aren't too good. We won't be able to outsmart her again like this."

"I hear horse drawn carriages," interrupted Henry Daly. "A lot of them."

"That will be all the Banshees from all over Ireland," said King Cormac. "The Banshee sent out messenger crows to announce the greatest departure celebration ever at the Cradle and she has invited all the Banshees to attend."

"We should get out of this dungeon area before the skeleguards show up to take us all away to departures," said King Brian. "Now is the time to make our move, no one is aware we have escaped, therefore no one is looking for us.

"Are we going to hide somewhere in the Banshee's Cradle?" asked Nanny wondering where could five leprechauns, two children, a dog and Santa Claus hide without being spotted.

"Actually Nanny Reilly," answered King Cormac, "we have some newfound allies in the Cradle who have extended an open invitation to us."

"We have?" said Nanny. "What are allies?"

"Friends," answered King Brian. "They're going to help us."

"What allies could we possibly have in the Cradle?" quizzed King Rory.

"There's no time to explain," answered King Brian. "Just follow me in single file and be as quiet as you possibly can. We'll explain when we get there."

The Rescueteers and Santa, led by King Brian with Henry Daly at the rear, as quickly and as quietly as possible made their way unnoticed through the Banshee's Cradle to their newfound allies. The underworld skeleguards were waiting at the secret trap door to escort them down the tunnel and into their brightly lit place of gathering. What a contrast for everyone. They go from the dismal cold dungeons of the Banshee's Cradle to a bright warm prestigious cave underground. They noticed how meticulously kept their surroundings were. The craftsmanship of the wooden table and chairs, and the detail in the hand sewn cushions on the seat of each chair. The perfect hand woven rug underneath the table. A chandelier with candles in each globe hung from the rock ceiling.

"Rescueteers, and Santa," said King Brian, "meet our allies. King Cormac and I were very fortunate to be caught by these two skeleguards after we came over the Cradle wall."

Nanny noticed they had a round table like their round mushroom. They had chairs to sit on and the Rescueteers had mushrooms. This must be the skeleguards official headquarters like Magandy's Pond is theirs. The skeleguards were lined up beside each other to greet Santa and the Rescueteers.

King Brian introduced everybody by name. "Meet Nanny Reilly, and her dog Henry Daly," Nanny smiled even though she was confused and a little scared. All the skeleguards looked alike, and all the skeleguards brought fear to Nanny. Henry Daly was also concerned, he didn't smile, he gave a low growl and stood very close to Nanny as he sensed her fear.

"This is Ned Franey," continued King Brian noticing Nanny's concern and Henry's protection mode.

"Hello," said Ned, he too was worried and shuffled forward to stand close to Henry Daly.

"This is my brother King Brendan of Ballyvaloo," said King Brian turning toward King Brendan.

"You both look identical," commented the lead skeleguard.

"So do you," answered King Brendan with a broad smile. "Are you brothers?"

"We're brothers in arms," answered the skeleguard as he patted his associate on the back. "Our mission is like yours, to outsmart the Banshee and escape from the Banshee's Cradle."

Nanny and Ned felt relieved when they heard the skeleguard say that. Now they weren't so scared. Henry Daly stood at ease beside Nanny and stopped his low growl.

"Meet my brother King Rory of Ballineskar and my lovely niece Princess Tara," said King Brian.

The skeleguards paused when it came to their turn to introduce each other.

"I'm afraid I can't introduce us like that. We don't have names. We just talk amongst each other without using names," said the lead skeleguard.

"Why don't you have names?" asked Nanny. This was strange she thought, Nanny had never met anyone without a name.

"We just don't," answered the lead skeleguard. "I believe once upon a time we had a name, but after we went through departures, we no longer had names. I became a skeleguard, my brother in arms became a skeleguard and my sister in arms became a skelassistant." He turned to the Banshee's skelassistant.

"Would you like to have a name?" asked Nanny.

The skelassistant stepped forward. "I'd like to have a name," she said.

"Can you think of a name you would like?" asked Princess Tara.

"I like all your names," answered the skelassistant. "Yours are the first names I've ever heard. I don't know any other names."

"Would you like me to give you a name?" asked Nanny.

"Yes," smiled the skelassistant, "I'd like that."

"You sound just like the seamstress who worked at the cleaners in town," said Nanny. Her name was Sadie Grady. Do you like the name Sadie Grady?" asked Nanny.

"Yes, I like the name Sadie Grady," answered the skelassistant. "Is that my name now?"

"If you like it, you can have it," said Nanny.

"My name is Sadie Grady," smiled the skelassistant. "My name is Sadie Grady."

Everybody smiled and agreed that Sadie Grady was a perfect name for the Banshee's skelassistant.

"Give me a name," requested the lead skeleguard. He didn't want to be left out.

"You sound just like Paddy Mac," said Ned. "He was a carpenter in the Bullring in town."

"Paddy Mac," said the skeleguard. "I like the name Paddy Mac—are you sure you want to give it to me?"

"Sure, you might as well have it," answered Ned. "I haven't seen Paddy Mac in ages. For all I know he could have left the country."

"And me too," said the other skeleguard. "What about a name for me?"

"We should call you Jimmy Finn," said Princess Tara. "Jimmy Finn was the only person to catch Uncle Brian and try to get the crock of gold from him, and you caught Uncle Brian tonight."

"Jimmy Finn," said the skeleguard, he turned to his comrades, "my name is Jimmy Finn. Jimmy Finn is my name. I have a name." The newly-christened comrades kept repeating their names to each other and themselves. It was the beginning of their new identity.

"It's a very fortunate coincidence that Jimmy Finn has caught me twice," said King Brian. "Now we have a hideout until the dust settles. Before we leave, we need to find that secret tunnel."

"Secret tunnel," repeated Santa.

"I'm afraid so," answered King Brian. "Show everybody what we discovered," he turned to his brothers.

King Brendan and King Rory opened the scrolls and spread them out on the floor for everybody to see. The Banshee's plans for all their villages was shocking news, but, if they could disable the wish-blocking device the Rescueteers could prevent the development plans from going forward.

"I know exactly where that is," said Sadie Grady, as she pointed to the X on the secret tunnel map. "It's directly under the skeledogs kennel. That's going to be very difficult to get to. These two particular skeledogs are vicious. They're never let out. Their job is to guard that secret tunnel and that's it. They sit in that kennel just waiting for something to move.

If anything at all catches their eye they jump against the kennel cage walls barking viciously, snarling and drooling. Everybody walks the long way around to their destination in case the skeledogs get out. No one gets in there only the Banshee, and she goes in alone."

Everything went quiet. How were they going to get to the secret tunnel? A new mission was upon them now. They had to think and act fast. There was no time at all for preparation. Was Coolrainy, Ballineskar, Ballyvaloo and Ballyconniger doomed? Were all the residents of these villages doomed also?

Nanny dropped her head. "If they scare all the skeletees, they're going to scare us too," she said sadly.

"They don't scare me," said Henry Daly, showing no fear. "You take us there Sadie Grady and I'll take care of the rest."

Nanny knelt beside Henry Daly and put her arms around him. "They scare me Henry Daly, what if they chew you up?" she said.

"They have to catch me first," said Henry in his scratchy voice with a big smile. "You're forgetting, my grandfather won the greyhound derby in record time. Those skeledogs don't stand a chance against me. Just open the kennel gate, stand back and I'll make sure they chase me."

"You're absolutely right Henry Daly," said Nanny. "They don't stand a chance of catching you. You keep them busy chasing you while we go into the secret tunnel to disarm the wish-blocking device. You're so clever."

"There's no dog as smart as Henry Daly," added Ned.

Everybody agreed, even Sadie Grady, Paddy Mac and Jimmy Finn.

"Good boy, Henry Daly," said King Brian as he proudly looked up at Henry. "You're also one of the bravest dogs in Ireland and I'm happy you're on our side."

Henry Daly smiled his bashful smile as Nanny continued to hug him.

"We should go right now," said King Brian, he made a move toward the exit. "It's probably best if some of us stay here, there's no need for all of us to go."

"If Henry Daly is going, I'm going said Nanny, she stood steadfast beside Henry.

"If Nanny is going, then I'm going," said Ned, he stood firm beside Nanny.

"If the children are going, I'm going," said Santa standing beside Ned. "I want to make sure they come back so I can give them their Christmas gifts, he winked at Nanny and Ned.

"I have to go to guide you to the tunnel," said Sadie Grady.

"You will need our help to open the skeledog's kennel gate," said Paddy Mac.

"That's very true, that kennel gate is very heavy, it will take Paddy Mac and me, Jimmy Finn to open it," said Jimmy Finn, happy for an opportunity to use his new name.

"I can't stay here," said Princess Tara. "I want to see Henry Daly run like the wind when he gets those mean skeledogs to chase him."

"I'm afraid, Brother Brian, if Tara is going, I need to go," said King Rory. "Need I say more?"

King Cormac turned to King Brendan, "Well, that just leaves the two of us, Brother Brendan," said King Cormac. "What do you think, should we go or should we stay?" "I'd hate to miss the greyhound derby, wouldn't you, Brother Cormac?" said King Brendan. "Especially when we have the odds on favorite and front row seats."

"We can't let Henry Daly down. Count us in, Brother Brian, we're going too," smiled King Cormac.

"Okay Rescueteers," said King Brian with a sigh and a smile, "let's complete our mission and get out of here."

The unusual looking entourage followed Sadie Grady down the hideout tunnel to make their way to the skeledog's kennel.

CHAPTER TWENTY- SEVEN

The Banshee's Cradle was busy. Skeleguards and skeletees from all departments were wandering toward Dreary Castle in small groups not paying attention to any of their surroundings. The news about the most prestigious departures of all time had spread throughout the Cradle and everybody was curious and wanted to sneak a peek.

One horse drawn carriage after the other was pulling into the Banshee's Cradle. The horses were attired in long black capes covered from head to hoof. Dreary Castle guest shuttle was written on the carriage doors. The Cradle Center had become a hive of activity. Large crow parking attendants were standing on hitching posts flapping their wings and cawing for parking business. Skeleguards were scrambling to find available hitching posts for their horses who were also clad in black attire like the carriage horses. Banshees galore in their black gowns were being escorted by other skeleguards to the departure terminal. It was exactly like that summer night when the original four Rescueteers were there before.

The Banshees were conversing amongst themselves as they made their way from the Cradle Center to departures. Heads were nodding and shoulders were shrugging. They were wondering who was going to be their entertainment for departures tonight? The possibilities were endless. There were a lot of mythical figures the Banshees showed a deep interest in over the years, but all these figures somehow managed to evade them.

All eight Rescueteers, Santa, Sadie Grady, Paddy Mac and Jimmy Finn were safely watching the high activity and keeping a low profile at the hidden entrance to the underworld hideout. In a few minutes the high drama will begin, then they will witness the results of their strategic planning.

"Who would have thought we would be back in this situation again?" whispered Nanny.

"I wouldn't have thought it," answered Ned quietly.

"Or me either," said Henry Daly.

"I would have bet the crock of gold against it," said King Brian. And you all know how leprechauns never want to give up the crock of gold."

"When I look at this scene with all these Banshees, skeleguards, crows, and horses in long black attires pulling Dreary Castle guest shuttles, my words could never describe it," added Santa.

"You're right," said Princess Tara, "as often as Uncle Brian has told this story about being in the Banshee's Cradle on that summer night, I would never have pictured this."

Finally, the last Banshee was escorted by the last skeleguard into Dreary Castle.

Dark lowly lit corridors led to departures. One hundred Banshees sat in ten rows of ten in high-backed skelechairs. The skeleguards arranged themselves around the perimeter of the departure terminal. They stood at ease with their skelehands behind their backs. The parking attendant crows left their hitching posts to eves drop on the occasion, they were perched in various nooks and crannies in the walls and the ceiling. Other skeletees did the same. They found dark corners, empty doorways and rafters, they lurked in the shadows awaiting this most prestigious departures of all time. The skelechef and his crew of skelecooks stood behind tall food carts at the swing doors to the kitchen. The departure door was center stage and all eyes were on it. Just before dawn a hush came over the departure terminal. All the mumbling and scuffling, the coughing, the laughing and giggling stopped. Silence filled the air. Not a sound was heard.

At that very moment, back in the Banshee's boudoir, the Banshee was sleeping so hard she was unaware of her guests arriving. She was still snoring away to her hearts content. The tin whistle from Nanny's checklist, which the Banshee has tossed across the room began to move. It teetered back and forth. Then it stood upright and rose into the air above the sleeping Banshee. It paused for a moment as though it was taking a breath and preparing itself for its own guest appearance. In an instant, without further ado, the melodious tone of the magnificent tin whistle filled the air and spread throughout the Cradle. Just as King Brendan had requested of the tin whistle at the break of dawn,

> "Oh Magic whistle
> Straight and tall
> Sure you're the sweetest
> Of them all.
> With your lilting tunes
> Of Carols bright
> Help us guide Santa
> Home tonight.
> As dawn awakes
> Stand upright
> And play your tune
> Silent Night.

The splendid tin whistle in the key of 'd' played its crisp precise notes,

> "So La So Mi,
> So La So Mi,
> Ray Ray Ti,
> Doe Doe So.
> La La Doe Ti La So La So Mi
> La La Doe Ti La So La So Mi.
> Ray Ray Faw Ray Ti Do Mi.
> Doe So Mi So Faw Ray Doe."

The Banshee's eyes suddenly opened wide. For a brief moment she stared wide eyed and in disbelief at the tin whistle hovering above her and serenading the silent night that it was.

She finally found her voice. "Music," screamed the Banshee, "in my boudoir, in my Cradle, in my world." She attempted to sit up but she couldn't. She twisted and try to turn and maneuver her body every way possible. She tried to kick up at the tin whistle with all her might.

No matter how hard she tried to twist and turn and kick she couldn't. "Skelassistant," she yelled. Skelassistant where are you? Skelassistant."

The Banshee's skelassistant no longer existed, she now had a new identity, Sadie Grady. Nobody came to the Banshee's rescue. Everybody was at the departure ceremony. The tin whistle floated across her boudoir, out the open door and down the dismal dark corridor still playing its beautiful melody.

Meanwhile, at the full house, floor to ceiling departure ceremony, the crystal clear notes of the tin whistle echoed throughout the terminal. All the Banshees sat lifeless. They too were in disbelief. Music. In the Banshee's Cradle. How horrific.

All the crows and skeletees were dumfounded. All eyes were still on the departure door. It opened wide and the floating lilting tin whistle made a grand entrance. It swooped through the air like an eagle in flight playing Silent Night and then gracefully left departures through the main entrance in the same grandioso style.

The Banshees were both horrified and disgusted. They abruptly left the departure terminal knocking over skelechairs as they left. They talked in disgust amongst themselves about the Banshee of Raven's Point. How could she play such a trick on her fellow Banshees?

The Skelechef and skelecooks looked around at each other. They never heard music before, but it seemed quite pleasant. They felt pleasant All the skeletees felt a change of energy. Nobody was in a hurry to leave departures right away. It seemed like they just wanted to absorb the moment.

"Here come the Banshees," said Nanny, "and they look upset."

"Oh I bet they're more than upset," said Princess Tara.

"Sure they don't appreciate good music, said King Brendan.

"They don't appreciate anything good at all," added King Rory.

The Rescueteers, together with Santa, Sadie Grady, Paddy Mac and Jimmy Finn were watching the hustle and bustle of the Cradle Center from their secluded spot.

The Banshees were rushing back to the Cradle Center which was now a hive of activity again. The escort skeleguards offered to help the Banshees into their carriages, but they refused any kind of assistance.

One Banshee stood on the step of her carriage and spoke to the others. "If the Banshee of Raven's Point thinks she can smooch her way back into our click she's mistaken." The rest of the Banshees cheered and applauded. "We'll never ever have anything to do with her again after that terrible trick she played on us," continued the visiting Banshee. "From now on, she's an outcast." The Banshees agreed never to darken the doorstep of the Banshee of Raven's Point again. She would never get another opportunity to trick them in any way ever again. Their black gowns caught the speed of the wind as they drove the carriages at a gallop out of the Banshee's Cradle never to return.

Unknown to the Rescueteers, at that very moment, back in the Banshee's boudoir, the Banshee had loosened the stitches. She was still twisting and kicking with all her might. One stitch after the other finally gave way and now the Banshee was free. Not only was she free, she was angrier than she had ever been in all her years of existence and somebody was going to pay for it.

CHAPTER TWENTY- EIGHT

"Follow me," said Sadie Grady. She kept her head down as she took lengthy strides and quietly led the way to the skeledog's kennel. Henry Daly stayed at the back of the group sniffing the air and watching out for anything moving.

Sadie Grady came to a halt behind a fallen dead pine tree. She didn't have to announce that the skeledogs were just a short distance ahead of them, they could be heard barking and snarling. The high activity in the Cradle Center had alerted them. The skeledogs were bouncing off the walls of the cage. They were more frightening than Sadie Grady had described. Nanny feared for Henry Daly, but Henry wasn't afraid, after all he was one of the bravest dogs in Ireland.

Paddy Mac and Jimmy Finn cautiously walked to the skeledog's kennel and nervously stood at the gate. Paddy Mac fumbled with the keys and let them fall. Jimmy Finn picked them up and tried one key after the other until he found the right key. The skeledogs continue to bounce of the cage walls making it difficult for Jimmy Finn to unlock the gate. Finally he got it and got ready to pull back the latch. Henry Daly placed himself just a length in front of the kennel gate. He got into his starting position and prepared himself for the race of his life. Nanny's heart was pounding. Henry was just one leap away from the skeledogs. She held her breath. Everybody held their breath.

Paddy Mac and Jimmy Finn nodded at Henry Daly letting him know they were ready. Henry nodded back, he too was ready. The skeledogs were furious. This was the worst they had ever been. Never before had anyone except the Banshee dared to come close to them. They were ready to tear Henry Daly apart. Paddy Mac and Jimmy Finn unlatched the gate and together they quickly pulled it back against them. The skeledogs came charging out at full speed. Henry Daly took off like a bullet and ran like the wind away from the kennel with the angry skeledogs snapping at his heels. He made the skeledogs follow him to the wall of the Cradle, he ran around the perimeter as though he was on a race track.

"Henry Daly will be fine Nanny," said Santa.

"I know he will," answered Nanny, "my brother Frank told me there's not a dog in the whole of Ireland faster than Henry Daly."

"Frank was right, Nanny," said Ned. "Look at Henry Daly go."

Everybody kept their eye on Henry, and from a distance as he raced around, he appeared to be smiling.

Sadie Grady pointed out the trap door to the secret tunnel. Paddy Mac and Jimmy Finn opened the trap door and offered to lead the Rescueteers down the tunnel. Nanny, Ned, King Brian, King Cormac, King Rory, Princess Tara, King Brendan and Santa followed in that order. Sadie Grady stayed behind as a lookout. She climbed a blackened pine tree close to the skeledog's kennel where she continued to watch Henry exhaust the skeledogs.

At the end of the secret tunnel the Banshee had many things of interest hidden. There were files that dated back to long before Nanny and Ned were born. There was a large chest of jewelry overflowing with pearl necklaces, gold bracelets, watches, rings broaches, earrings, any piece of jewelry you could imagine in silver and gold. Beside that was another large chest with silks of all descriptions in scarves, handkerchiefs, neckties, shirts and blouses.

"Jeepers," said Nanny, "Tommy Riordan was right. He said Long John Silver's treasure was buried at Raven's Point."

"This is not Long John Silver's treasure, Nanny," said Santa. "These are all the jewels and silks from the victims of the Banshee. This is now the Banshee's treasure."

"I'm glad the Banshee is tied up." said King Brian. "If she caught us in here, in her secret tunnel with all her secret treasures she would surely skin us alive. We need to find that wish-blocking device and get out of here fast," said King Brian. Shivers went down his spine thinking of the possibility of her showing up unannounced.

"It seems the Banshee went to great efforts to put this secret tunnel together," said Santa as he studied the walls. "She built up the walls with nice red bricks,"

"Those red bricks look familiar," said King Brian, remembering the struggle Princess Tara, himself and the other leprechaun Kings had to remove one brick to retrieve a bunch of keys,

"Perhaps there's a loose brick or two in this wall also with a secret behind it," said King Brendan.

"Let's pound on each brick," added Princess Tara, she kicked at one of the bricks, "I bet there is a loose one."

"I'll check the rows from my waist up on this wall," said Santa as he looked down at his shorter associates. Paddy Mac and Jimmy Finn checked the bricks on the other walls at the same level as Santa, while Nanny and Ned tapped on the bricks from their knee level and above. King Brian, King Brendan, King Cormac and Princess Tara checked the bricks from the ground up to as far as they could reach. Everyone was tapping away, brick by brick, row by row, until Santa finally tapped on a loose brick.

"Over here," he said with excitement. "This might be the loose brick we're looking for."

Everybody gathered round and saw the loose brick Santa found. He teased at the brick and pulled it out. Behind the brick there was a bony handle attached to the wall. Beside the handle were two arrows, one said fog on the other said fog off. This made no sense to anyone. They expected to see wish-blocking device on and wish-blocking device off. Underneath the handle was a scroll. Santa unrolled the scroll and read the words,

This wish-blocking device,
Is oh so nice.
Leprechaun wishes no more.
The fog of the Cradle
Will always disable,
The wish as it comes through the door.
This wish-blocking device,
Is oh so nice,
Christmas wishes no more.
No Santa, no cheer,
No gifts to share
Only Christmas tears galore.

"This is it," said Santa, all we have to do is turn off the fog and then we can go home and Christmas will begin.

"Hurray," yelled all the Rescueteers in unison.

As Santa reached for the bony handle to turn off the fog an old boot came flying at him, hit him on the head and knocked him down.

He heard that familiar wicked voice "You should have left when you had the chance Mr. Santa Claus, ha ha ha."

Everybody turned around in fear. The Banshee was blocking the tunnel exit. There was no way out and she had an unsuspecting Princess Tara held tightly in her bony fist. Princess Tara wanted to punch out at her but she couldn't free her arms, the Banshee's grip was too tight.

"All of you move away from that switch," said the Banshee. "If you don't, I'll crush this silly little leprechaun girl with my bare hand." She slowly squeezed her fist and Princess Tara cried out in pain.

"We're moving, don't hurt her," said King Rory as he ushered everyone away from the switch.

"Keep moving to the exit," said the Banshee as she moved toward them. "We're going back to departures, but now I have a different plan in store for all of you, all except this one." She squeezed Princess Tara, and once again Princess Tara cried out in pain.

"Take me instead of her," pleaded King Rory as he took a step toward the Banshee.

"Stay back," yelled the Banshee, she was furious. Her eyes were wide and and her face was tight, she held up Princess Tara "You stupid silly leprechaun," she said to King Rory, "if you take one more step toward me I'll make her suffer dearly.

Princess Tara was beginning to weaken under the pressure of the Banshee's grip. The Rescueteers, Santa, Paddy Mac and Jimmy Finn did exactly as the Banshee said. They knew the Banshee would crush Princess Tara in an instant she was so mad, they moved toward the tunnel exit.

"I see now how you fooled me," said the Banshee as she squinted and stared the four leprechaun kings up and down. "Two sets of twins. What a clever existence you have all lived for all these years. But now those days are gone. None of you will ever exist again."None of the Kings responded to the Banshee. They made no clever remarks, if they did Princess Tara would suffer dearly.

"You two," said the Banshee as she pointed at Paddy Mac and Jimmy Finn, "you betrayed me. Your heads will roll."

Paddy Mac and Jimmy Finn showed no fear and offered no excuses. They didn't volunteer to be skeletees at the Banshee's Cradle, therefore they didn't betray her. In fact, the Banshee was the one who betrayed them. Santa also kept quiet. None of them had any bargaining power with the Banshee. At this point, one simple word could infuriate her to the point of disaster for Princess Tara.

Nanny and Ned were more terrified now than earlier when the skeleguards caught them at the west side wall. King Brian and King Cormac were not going to rescue them now. They didn't make a strategic escape plan for this capture at Magandy's Pond. They couldn't strut their way out of this one, they only had one hope now, and that was Henry Daly.

CHAPTER TWENTY-NINE

Henry Daly had out ran the two skeledogs and left them flat out exhausted at the other side of the Banshee's Cradle. He quickly made his way back to the skeledog's kennel to join all his comrades. When he got there, no one was to be seen anywhere.

"They must still be in that secret tunnel," he said. "I'll find them." He sniffed at the ground and made his way to the tunnel entrance. He suddenly stopped as he caught the scent of the Banshee. Could she possibly be in there, or was she here earlier? He heard a sound from above.

"Psst, psst, Henry Daly." Henry looked above him and saw Sadie Grady high up in a tree holding onto a dead branch for dear life.

"The Banshee caught all your friends; she's in the secret tunnel with them now," said Sadie Grady in a loud whisper.

"Everybody," replied Henry Daly.

"Everybody," answered Sadie Grady, "even Paddy Mac and Jimmy Finn. She's surely going to turn the two of them into table legs and skelechairs."

"And Nanny and Ned, all my friends and Santa too," said Henry Daly. "She's not going to have them as skeletees now after they escaped and made a fool out of her."

"What are we going to do?" asked Sadie Grady, who had no ideas whatsoever.

"We have to have a plan," answered Henry Daly remembering when he, Nanny Ned and Princess Tara wanted to take off straight away to rescue Santa with no plan, "and we have to think fast, those skeledogs will be back as soon as they get their breath back."

Henry paused and began some serious thinking. He knew the safety of the Rescueteers and their newfound allies was most important. He also knew King Brian said he was good to have on their side because not only was he a fine Rescueteer, but he also had speed and agility, he could also be ferocious and scary too. If they did get into any kind of difficulty, Henry Daly would be the anchor dog and keep the Banshee and her cronies at bay until the Rescueteers escaped.

"I know what we should do," said Henry Daly. "We'll let the Banshee send everyone out of the tunnel. She's not going to lead them out because she has to keep an eye on them all. She's going to be the last one out of the tunnel, that's when we'll make our move and separate her from the Rescueteers, Santa, Paddy Mac and Jimmy Finn."

"Our move," said Sadie Grady, still clinging to the dead branch of the tree.

"You'll have to come down from that tree and get ready to run for your life when they come out of the tunnel, otherwise you're going to be left behind," said Henry Daly smiling up at Sadie Grady and showing his teeth.

Sadie Grady quickly made her way down the tree. She inhaled and exhaled and ran on the spot for a moment. She began stretching and then twisting herself from the waist. Her bones creaked a little. "I'm preparing myself for a mad dash," she said to Henry Daly. "These bones haven't operated like that in a while so I'm giving them a quick reminder on flexibility, I hope they make it out of here."

When Henry heard the creaking of Sadie Grady's bones he too hoped she would make it out of there in one piece.

"Shh," said Henry Daly, "I hear them. Get ready to run."

Sadie Grady jogged 100 yards away from the skeledog's kennel and ran in a small circle to stay limbered up. She then got in the starting position with one leg stretched out in front of the other, her bony body slightly bent over and her arms ready to propel her full steam ahead out of the Cradle. She was as ready as she would ever be.

Henry Daly waited behind the skeledog's kennel. The first one out of the tunnel was Nanny and she saw Sadie Grady looking straight ahead bent over in the starting position. Nanny slightly paused, but didn't say a word. She looked behind her to Ned and pointed Sadie Grady out to him. Ned too paused, they both wondered what Sadie Grady was doing. Ned looked around to see if there was any other strange behaving skeletees. When he looked to his right his eyes opened wide and he slightly paused again. He saw Henry Daly at the kennel with his paw to his mouth, indicating to Ned not to say a word. Ned nodded at Henry and tapped Nanny on her right shoulder, she looked over her shoulder and reacted wide-eyed like Ned. Henry Daly still had his paw to his mouth.

King Brian was next out of the tunnel, King Rory, King Brendan and King Cormac. They didn't see Sadie Grady ahead of them they were too short for that, but they certainly saw Henry Daly. As soon as they saw him they knew what his plan was. He was going to pounce on the Banshee. But what about Princess Tara? Henry had no idea the Banshee had such a tight grasp on the little Princess.

"Keep moving," yelled the Banshee from inside the tunnel. "Why have you slowed down? I can become a bone crusher in an instant." Princess Tara let out another cry of pain. Everybody walked faster.

Henry's ears pricked up. He heard Princess Tara cry out. Now he knew the Banshee had her in some sort of way. The hackles on the back of his neck stood up. He began foaming from the mouth, he was as mad as he could possibly be. How dare the Banshee hurt Princess Tara.

Paddy Mac and Jimmy Finn followed the leprechaun Kings. They could see Sadie Grady ahead of them. They knew the Banshee was capable of many things, so they thought the Banshee had stopped Sadie Grady in her tracks and turned her into a statue. What other reason could there possibly be for this intent stillness. Then to add to their surprise they saw Henry Daly behind the kennel foaming at the mouth. If they didn't know better, Henry would certainly pass for any of the two skeledogs he lured away.

Santa was the last of the comrades to exit the tunnel and because he was so well tuned into human behavior, he noticed everything at a glance. He saw Sadie Grady ready to run, Nanny and Ned pausing, everybody looking to the right noticing something but saying nothing. From what Santa saw he knew Henry Daly was there. He also knew in the next five seconds Henry would need his help saving Princess Tara.

The Banshee came out of the tunnel still holding on tight to Princess Tara. She was taking brisk strides behind her captors. Santa suddenly dropped his body to the ground making the Banshee trip over him.

"Ahh," cried the Banshee as she tripped and fell facedown. She was unable to keep her tight hold on Princess Tara and let her go. The little Princess was hurled through the air. Henry Daly quickly leaped forward and carefully with his teeth caught Princess Tara by the fine green riding jacket she was wearing. He placed her gently on the ground and gave her one of his bright smiles. Santa quickly stood to his feet and sat on the Banshee before she could get up. Sadie Grady heard all the commotion and without looking over her shoulder took off running as fast as her two skeletal legs could carry her.

"Get off me, you're crushing me," screamed the Banshee. She was kicking her feet as hard and as fast as she could. She tried to move her body, she huffed and puffed and gasped in her struggles, but Santa was too heavy. All the comrades except Sadie Grady, turned to see what was happening.

Santa sprang up and down on the Banshee's back. "It's not a pleasant thing to be crushed Banshee, is it?" said Santa. "Now you know how little Princess Tara felt." He shifted his body to emphasize his weight again. "Perhaps you should also know what it feels like to be caged."

"You aren't caging me," screamed the Banshee as she got a new burst of energy. She beat the ground with her fists and kicked her feet as fast and as hard as she could.

"Oh yes we are," said Santa as he stood and grabbed the Banshee's left leg to drag her to the skeledog's cage. Jimmy Finn and Paddy Mac quickly grabbed her other wildly kicking leg. Nanny and Ned rushed to help Santa. The Banshee tried grasping any kind of foliage she could to hold on to. But everything was so dead and withered it uprooted very quickly. Her long fingernails dug into the ground and created rivets in the dirt as she was being dragged along.

"Don't you dare put me in a cage. Don't you dare. I'll make you all pay dearly for this," she screamed as she continued to kick and claw at the dirt.

Nanny and Ned were struggling to hold on to the Banshee's wrestling leg with Santa, but they refused to let go. Henry Daly with Princess Tara on his back, was nose to nose with the Banshee snarling and drooling. He was not going to let her fight and kick her way out of this. Princess Tara was thrilled to see the Banshee under captivity.

"You mean old witch," said Princess Tara, I told you, you would be sorry."

King Brian and King Brendan, held the cage gate open wide as the Banshee was been dragged through. King Rory and King Cormac assisted at the gate by tapping on the Banshee's bony knuckles with their shillelaghs when the Banshee grabbed the walls of the cage. Nanny, Ned, Santa, Jimmy Finn and Paddy Mac let go of the Banshee and left the cage ina hurry. King Brian and King Brendan slammed the cage door shut and Santa quickly bolted it. The Banshee was now, for the very first time in her existence, in captivity. She yelled at everyone and shook the cage vigorously.

"I'll get you again Mr. Santa Claus, don't you think you have seen the last of me, and you too all you silly leprechauns," she cried. "Nanny Reilly and Ned Franey, I'll remember you two and that dog of yours. As for you two traitor skeleguards, I'll make you pay dearly."

Santa turned his back to the Banshee. His large frame blocked her out. "Pay no attention to anything she says," he said, "Never again will the Banshee ever harm any of us. Now, where were we before we were rudely interrupted?" said Santa as he rubbed his head where the Banshee's old boot hit him.

It was agreed by all concerned, that Henry Daly and King Brian should go back down the tunnel to turn off the wish-blocking device switch while the rest of the comrades made their way as fast as they could to King Brendan's ladder.

CHAPTER THIRTY

Jimmy Finn quickly and carefully led the way, just as he had when he caught King Brian and King Cormac. He knew the safe and hidden route to take. He was followed by a still scared and tired Nanny and Ned. They had hoped this long night would be well over by now and they were safely snuggled up in their warm and comfortable beds to awaken on Christmas Eve morning with the Banshee's Cradle behind them. They could still hear the Banshee's angry yells in the distance as they got further and further away from her. They were followed by Santa with Princess Tara sitting on his right shoulder. The little princess was still tired and feeling the effects of the Banshee's grip on her. So Santa put her on his shoulder to rest. King Rory took advantage of Santa's left shoulder, while King Brendan and King Cormac under Santa's kind persuasion fit nicely into his red jacket pockets. Paddy Mac took Henry Daly's position at the rear of the line and kept a close watch on their surroundings, after all, if a skeleguard was going to surprise them, he knew the most likely areas this would happen.

Nanny didn't like being separated from Henry Daly. She kept looking behind her hoping to see him gallop up behind them with King Brian on his back. She knew they weren't out of the woods yet, and it was always a comforting feeling to have her loyal companion on guard at her side. She feared for him and King Brian. She also knew it was only a matter of time before the skeleguards would discover the loose skeledogs and hear the cries of the Banshee coming from their cage.

The morning sun had risen and daylight spread throughout the Banshee's Cradle. The darkness no longer hid them. Just as they were coming close to King Brendan's ladder, Jimmy Finn made a sudden stop and lay flat out on the ground. Without saying a word, he gestured to everybody to get down and keep perfectly still. He could hear twigs snapping close by. Were they been followed? Paddy Mac signaled to Jimmy Finn that he was going to circle around the blackened pines and come up behind the unsuspecting culprit. He crept away on his haunches and disappeared out of sight. Not a word was said among the waiting comrades. Several minutes went by and not a sound was heard anywhere. Where was Paddy Mac? Why wasn't he back by now?

Nanny could feel something move underneath her elbow. She lifted her arm and saw a small sprig of a pine tree with green pine needles on it. That's the first piece of green I've seen in the Banshee's Cradle, she thought. The floor of the Cradle began to shimmer. A lot of things were moving underneath them and beneath the soil as they lay in wait for Paddy Mac to return.

"I'm scared Nanny," whispered Ned, trembling.

"I'm scared too, Ned," replied Nanny. "I'm not sure if we should run for it or not."

Jimmy Finn was scared too. His bones began to rattle. He gestured to everyone to come toward him. Santa, with Princess Tara and King Rory now sitting on his back, elbowed his way up beside Nanny and Ned. King Brendan and King Cormac crawled behind him.

"Gather round, everybody," said Jimmy Finn. "There's something very strange happening. I've never witnessed brightness and the earth moving like this in the Cradle before, and Paddy Mac should be back by now. I think you should all get out of here now while you can."

"But what about Henry Daly?" said Nanny. "I can't leave Henry Daly behind."

"And Uncle Brian," said Princess Tara, "we have to wait here for them."

"I'll wait here," said Jimmy Finn, but all of you should go now as fast as your two legs will carry you."

The earth began to move like ripples in the ocean. Small sprigs of pine trees and fern broke through the soil.

"Look at this," said Santa, "a sign of life." He was staring at a tiny purple wildflower growing right under his nose as he lay on the ground.

"And look at this," said King Rory as he lay face down. "A shamrock growing before my very eyes."

"And a bluebell growing before my very eyes," added King Cormac.

"Hey, look at me," laughed Princess Tara, a beautiful lush green fern leaf lifted Princess Tara from Santa's back and carefully placed her on the ground.

"Ha, ha," laughed King Rory as a lush green fern leaf lifted him from Santa's back and stood him beside Princess Tara

Nanny and Ned were also laughing hard. A pine tree had grown from the ground and two of the branches gently wrapped themselves around Nanny and Ned and carefully stood them beside Princess Tara and King Rory. Another pine tree grew in the same fashion and offered a limb to Santa to help him up, and then brushed the loose twigs and forest debris from Santa's red cloak with several of its branches.

"Ho, ho, ho," laughed Santa as he looked up to the sky with the palms of his hands turned up. "It's snowing twinkle dust."

Two toadstools grew under King Cormac and King Brendan giving them two seats to sit on. They too laughed hard.

The earth slowly tore itself open and new fresh ferns and pine trees grew to maturity in minutes. The forest floor covered itself in bluebells, purple, yellow and white wildflowers. Lush green grass, shamrocks and clover leaves. Birds could be heard singing and seen flying overhead.

"Look at me everybody, look at me," Jimmy Finn cried. "I have meat on my bones, I have a face." Jimmy Finn was touching his face. He had a nose and eyebrows, cheeks and lips. He didn't look like a skeleguard anymore, he looked like a normal human being wearing a nice shirt and trousers.

"Jimmy Finn," said everybody, they were flabbergasted. What a shocking surprise.

"He's not the only one with meat on his bones," Paddy Mac's voice made its way into the laughter and exhilaration of Santa the Rescueteers and Jimmy Finn. Paddy Mac strolled into the crowd, he was wearing a nice shirt and corduroy trousers with a beautiful Sadie Grady at his side.

"We're all normal human beings just like we wanted to be," said a tearful Sadie Grady. "I don't know how to thank you all. She wore a pretty red jacket, she had long thick black wavy hair, very fine facial features and a beautiful smile.

The ground began to tremble again and the sound of a loud engine could be heard coming toward them, what could this possibly be?

"Hide everybody," yelled Santa. "This could be trouble coming toward us,"

Without wasting a moment everybody hid behind the magnificent pine trees and waited for the engine intruder.

"It sounds like the SkelOrientation Express said Jimmy Finn. "I've heard that sound often enough."

"The skelegineers are probably out looking for us," added Paddy Mac, his anger showing on his round face. "There's no way I'm going back to the way I was, they aren't going to catch me."

"Or me either," said Sadie Grady, still tearful. "We're getting out of here and we are going to live like human beings,"

"It's the SkelOrientation Express," said Ned. "But it looks different, like new."

"It's red and yellow," said Nanny, "and it has The Liberty Express written on it."

"And it's full of people," said Santa. "What's going on?"

"All aboard," yelled a familiar scratchy voice from The Liberty Express as the smokestack puffed out perfect circles of white smoke.

"It's Henry Daly, it's Henry Daly," cried Nanny jumping and waving for joy.

"Henry Daly, we're over here." Henry had his head out the engineer's window with a big bright smile on his face and his tongue hanging out.

"And Uncle Brian," cried Princess Tara, "Uncle Brian." She was waving as hard as she could and jumping up and down.

"Next stop, Coolrainy," yelled King Brian as he stuck his head out the engineer's window beside Henry Daly.

"Hurrah for King Brian and Henry Daly," cried Ned. "We can go home."

"Hallelujah," said Santa with tears in his eyes, "what a wonderful Christmas this is going to be."

The Liberty Express came to a slow halt. It was a beautiful sight. The engine and the carriages were a shiny fire engine red with bright yellow trim. The words The Liberty Express on the sides of the engine and every carriage door were also a bright yellow. People were looking out gold framed windows and waving with delight.

"It's all the skeletees," said Sadie Grady. "We're all human beings again," she continued to cry tears of joy.

Henry Daly jumped off the train and ran toward Nanny. Nanny locked her arms around him. "You did it, Henry Daly," she said. "You did it, you turned off the wish-blocking device and made a wish."

Henry was so excited to see Nanny he wiggled out of her locked arms and began licking her all over her face. Nanny was laughing hard. Ned knelt beside Nanny and hugged Henry Daly, Henry was thrilled to see Ned too and licked him all over his face. Nanny, Ned, and Henry Daly were exhilarated. They rolled around the forest floor laughing.

King Brian jumped off the train. "Three cheers for the Rescueteers," he yelled. "Hip hip, hurrah. Hip hip, hurrah. Everybody cheered, even the x-skeletees.

King Brendan, King Cormac, King Rory and Princess Tara ran toward King Brian. Princess Tara jumped up in his arms. "You're the most clever leprechaun Ireland has ever known Uncle Brian," she said as she hugged him tight.

"You're absolutely right, lass," answered King Brian with his cock of the walk smile. "Sure, haven't I been telling you that for years?"

All four leprechaun kings laughed. That was an absolute fact. King Brian possessed an extra twinkle in his eye and grit in his heart whenever a daunting task lay ahead of him.

When he and Henry Daly returned down the tunnel to turn off the wish-blocking device, he knew this had to be their last hurrah. He knew there was no more coming back to the Banshee's Cradle. Therefore, not only did they have to get the Rescueteers and Santa out, they also had to get all the skeletees and skeledogs out too. After all, isn't that what the Rescueteers are all about, for the good of mankind and animal kind.

Henry Daly stood on his hind legs and leaned against the red brick wall where the wish-blocking device switch was. King Brian stood on Henry Daly's head and pulled down on the switch. As he did so, he took a deep breath, closed his eyes tight and said the words,

> "May all that is right happen tonight.
> May all that is wrong go away.
> May the Banshee and her Cradle no longer exist.
> May a new forest be born today.
> May the skeletees transform back to their norm.
> May the skeledogs do the same.
> As they came in, may they go out
> On the new Liberty Express Train."

King Brian opened his eyes and twinkle dust glittered in the air. It was then both he and Henry Daly knew everything was going to be just fine. Henry Daly with King Brian on his back left the tunnel to join their comrades in style on the SkelOrientation Express.

CHAPTER THIRTY-ONE

After all the jubilation, the transformation of the Banshee's Cradle and skeletees, the arrival of The Liberty Express, the hugs, the laughter, the cheers and the tears, everybody boarded the train. The old skelengineers, who were now human engineers took over the engine, blew the whistle and slowly the train began rolling its way out of the Cradle. The passengers cheered and applauded. Former skeledogs of all colors, shapes and sizes, some with their heads out the carriage windows, let out happy barks galore. They were free of the Banshee and her dark world. The Rescueteers, Santa, Paddy Mac, Jimmy Finn and Sadie Grady sat in the end carriage and looked back at what was once a dark and scary desolate place. They were now in awe at its vibrant beauty. A peaceful silence surrounded them as they reflected on the night of fear and horror they just went through.

The Liberty Express stopped at, what was once the main entrance to the Cradle. The gates were now gone and the whole forest came together. Bertie and Frosty were still tethered to the lowly branches of the pine trees. So too were King Brian's white horse, King Rory's grey horse, King Cormac's black horse and King Brendan's spirited chestnut mare. They were calmly grazing on lush green grass. It was a peaceful and uneventful night for them.

"I want to ride Frosty home," said Nanny, she was so happy to see her lovely white pony. Frosty looked at Nanny and whinnied, she was happy to see Nanny too.

"Well then, I'm going to ride Bertie home," said Ned. Ned too was thrilled to see Bertie and Bertie was happy to see Ned. He tossed his head up and down as if to say to Ned, "Let's go for a ride."

"I think we should all ride back to Magandy's Pond," said Santa. "After all, morning has broken and it's now Christmas Eve. I have a special gift for you all and I would like to give it to you at the official headquarters of the Rescueteers."

Nanny and Ned nudged each other. A special gift from Santa. What could it be? This is why Christmas was always Nanny's most favorite time of the year, apart from having no school, Santa was always going to surprise her no matter what.

"I'm going to ride Rudolph to Magandy's Pond," said Santa.

"But Rudolph is not here," said Ned.

"Well, we'll soon remedy that," smiled Santa, "especially now that leprechaun wishes and Christmas wishes are back in full swing." He winked at his captive audience and he too had the same twinkle in his eye that King Brian had. Santa stepped off The Liberty Express and took three giant steps away from the train. He twitched his nose and his red Santa hat with white furry trim appeared on his head. "That feels much better," he smiled.

The Rescueteers got off the train to be closer to Santa and see him bring Rudolph to the forest. Santa's feeling of Christmas Magic had come back to him and all he had to do was think of his reindeer before him, and in an instant, there he was. Rudolph with his magnificent buffed out antlers and his shiny red nose, his gold bells and his slick shined leather reins, saddle bags and a shiny leather headset. Rudolph was a beautiful sight.

"Ho, ho, ho," said Santa in his burly voice. He patted Rudolph on the neck and then gave him a big Santa hug. "It's so good to see you, Rudolph. You look magnificent."

"He's so big," said Ned, noticing how wide and tall Rudolph was compared to Bertie and Frosty, not to mention the Kings miniature horses.

His nose is really red," said Princess Tara as she stood under Rudolph's nose and stared at it.

This was a habit Rudolph was well used to by now, his nose for his entire life was a real eye catcher.

"I wish it was a night sky," said Nanny. "Then we would really see how bright Rudolph's nose shines."

No sooner were the words out of Nanny's mouth, when the sky darkened and filled with stars. Rudolph's nose got brighter and brighter and the surrounding area had a red glow to it.

"Jeepers," said Nanny, "I forgot I could wish again."

Everybody laughed and well understood Nanny's words. They all forgot they could wish again.

Sadie Grady stepped off the Liberty Express into the red glow of the now night sky. Paddy Mac and Jimmy Finn followed her. This for them was goodbye. Their eyes filled with tears as they thanked and hugged Santa and the Rescueteers. They now had a name and a brain and were ready to celebrate Christmas as ordinary people. They had a life to go back to and promised to keep in touch. What a great Christmas gift for them and all the other Liberty Express passengers. As the Liberty Express chugged away from the Rescueteers and Santa, Sadie Grady, Paddy Mac and Jimmy Finn from the last carriage continued to wave goodbye until they got out of sight.

Nanny was sad to see them disappear. Santa noticed Nanny's sadness.

"Don't worry Nanny Reilly," said Santa. "I'll be paying them a visit tonight, and I have a special gift for them too. They, just like the rest of us are going to have a wonderful Christmas."

Nanny smiled and realized she would see them again in Coolrainy. That made her feel better.

"Let's go home," said King Rory as he put his arm around Princess Tara.

"What wonderful words," smiled King Brian. "Let's go home."

Everybody agreed, and with a smile and a sigh repeated the words to themselves, "Let's go home."

Nanny and Ned ran to Bertie and Frosty. Princess Tara jumped on Henry Daly's back and the four leprechaun Kings mounted their trusty steeds.

Santa was not so agile. He turned to Rudolph and said, "I'm going to need a little help from you my friend."

Rudolph understood the help Santa needed, so he knelt on the forest floor and made it easy for Santa to get on his back.

"I'm ready whenever you are," he said in his deep calm voice. He picked up his leather reins and cried, "Onward Rudolph, Up Up and away." Rudolph in a single bound was air born. "Ho, ho, ho," laughed Santa.

Nanny tightened the stampede cord on her cowboy hat. "<u>Up</u> <u>Up</u> and <u>away</u> <u>Frosty</u>," she cried with delight.

Ned too tightened his stampede cord. "<u>Up</u> <u>Up</u> and <u>Away</u> <u>Bertie</u>," he yelled out at the top of his voice.

"<u>Up</u> <u>Up</u> and <u>away</u> <u>Henry Daly</u>," cried Princess Tara as she held on to Henry's scruff for dear life.

King Brian quickly gathered his brothers together. "There's one thing missing before we take off," he said smiling.

"What's that, Brother Brian?" asked King Brendan.

"A little Christmas music," answered King Brian. With that, he snapped his fingers in the air and the infamous tin whistle in the key of 'd' appeared hovering above their heads.

"Oh lilting whistle,
Up, up and away,
Pick a tune,
And let's hear you play."

Rudolph's bells were jingling as he and Santa took off. The tin whistle tuned into the bells, and as it did before, inhaled and in an instant began its jingle bell notes of yuletide joy.

"Mi Mi Mi,
Mi Mi Mi,
Mi So Do Re Mi.
Fa Fa Fa,
Fa Fa Mi Mi,
Mi Mi Mi Re,
Re Mi Re.
So, Mi Mi Mi,
Mi Mi Mi,
Mi So Do Re Mi,
Fa Fa Fa,
Fa Fa Mi, Mi,
Mi Mi So So Fa Re Do."

The Rescueteers and Santa all sang along at the top of their voices,

"Jingle bells
Jingle bells
Jingle all the way.
Oh what fun
It is to ride
On a one horse
Open sleigh.
Oh, Jingle bells
Jingle bells
Jingle all the way,
Oh what fun
It is to ride
On an open sleigh tonight.

As the Rescueteers flew over Katie's field, they could see the sparkle of Bull Cullen's four-foot-tall Christmas tree. Twinkle dust was falling on it like shining snowflakes. Nanny and Ned could see their prized possessions still under the little tree with Bull Cullen's. It was a wonderful welcome home for all. They landed at Magandy's Pond out of breath and overwhelmed with joy. The Rescueteers dismounted and once again Rudolph accommodated Santa with his dismount. Santa's legs were a little stiff and wobbly, it had been quite a few years since he rode a reindeer. He looked around at Magandy's Pond. What a lovely sight in the red glow of Rudolph's nose.

"Magandy's Pond always looks so peaceful," he said.

"Do you fish here too?" asked Nanny wondering why she never saw Santa here, "this is where the biggest rocheens are."

"I caught a huge one yesterday," added Ned, then his red freckled face frowned. "I threw it back in over there, but I should have kept it, because nobody believed me when I told them how big it was."

"For some strange reason when you catch a big fish," said King Brendan, "it's best to keep it so people can see it with their own eyes. Otherwise, you didn't catch it."

"But Ned did catch it," said Nanny. "I saw it—it was huge."

"I'm sure the fish was huge, Nanny Reilly," smiled Santa, "but there are certain things in life, and a big fish happens to be one of them, adults especially have to see it before they believe it."

"Sure aren't we a fine example of that," said Princess Tara with her hand on her hip. "There are some people who don't believe in leprechauns and here we're as real as can be."

"And what about me?" said Santa. "Don't you think I'm as real as can be as I stand here with Rudolph before your very eyes? But yet, I'm sorry to say I have quite a few nonbelievers."

"I didn't see the big fish Ned caught," added Henry Daly in support of Ned with his notorious smile. "I was busy scouting through the reeds, but I believe Ned."

"I know what we should do," said Nanny excitedly. "Let's make a Christmas wish that people believe in what they don't see."

"Ho, ho, ho Nanny Reilly," laughed Santa as he looked at Nanny over the rim of his gold framed glasses. "That's an interesting idea. How about we keep a little mystery about us, and leave them all guessing?"

"I like that idea," said King Brian. "A little mystery is a good thing." His eye twinkled. "Now you see me—" King Brian suddenly disappeared but his voice and laughter could still be heard. "And now you don't, ha ha.

Everybody joined in on King Brian's laughter and agreed a little mystery really was a good thing. Magandy's Pond was aglow not only with Rudolph's shiny nose, but with the laughter from the Rescueteers and Santa.

CHAPTER THIRTY-TWO

After the laughter settled down and King Brian reappeared, Santa paused and looked at each of the Rescueteers. "Nanny Reilly, Ned Franey, Henry Daly, Princess Tara, King Brian, King Rory, King Brendan and King Cormac. My dear good friends," he said, in his deep soft voice, "I'll be indebted to you for life. You risked yourselves for me. He leaned over and looked Nanny, Ned and Princess Tara in the eye. "Without doubt," he continued, "you're the bravest children in Ireland and are a credit to the human race. Therefore, I have a special keepsake for you all. He stood tall and retrieved a small red and gold box from Rudolph's saddle bags. He then removed a small gold key from the leather pouch on his belt. He opened the red and gold box with the golden key and handed a gold medallion hanging from a finely spun gold thread to Nanny. "Every Christmas, when you hang this on your tree, you will remember this Christmas and how special it was."

Nanny stared at it. "That looks like my head engraved into the medallion," said Nanny.

"It is you," replied Santa with a smile all across his rosy red cheeks

"I look so nice," she said. "Even my hair looks nice." Nanny touched her hair around her ears, of course it had long dried and was now sticking out under her hat as it was on the gold medallion. "I never saw me engraved into anything before. I only see other people's heads on coins."

Santa laughed at Nanny. "That's because they're special people and now you are too Nanny Reilly, all of you are. And a special dog." Santa acknowledged Henry Daly.

"Look at the other side," he said.

Nanny turned it over, and an inscription engraved into the back of the medallion in beautiful italics read, 'Nanny Reilly, Christmas prevails because of you, Forever in your debt, Your friend always, Santa.' Nanny held on tight to her gold medallion, this really was a keepsake for life. Santa gave one to Ned with him engraved into it and the same inscription on the back.

"Now my head is famous too," said Ned as he admired his profile and rubbed his thumb over his engraved image.

Henry Daly got one too and he held it between his two front paws. "I look like a Derby winner," smiled Henry. "If my grandfather saw my head on this he would be so proud of me."

"This is such a special gift," said King Brian, overwhelmed and tearful as he admired his own profile on the medallion and read the heartwarming words engraved on the back from Santa. "I don't know what to say."

Princess Tara handed her Uncle Brian her tiny handkerchief. He wiped his eyes and thanked Santa from the bottom of his heart.

"I often wondered why the head of a leprechaun kings wasn't on any Irish coin," said King Brendan. "Now I know why."

"And why would that be, Brother Brendan?" asked King Cormac.

"Sure there's no room on them for such a fine head, all the coins are too small," answered King Brendan. "A head as fine as that needs room to be shown off." He held up his medallion to show everybody his fine profile.

"You're absolutely right, Brendan," said King Rory, who couldn't take his eyes off his own profile. "I never realized we were so regal-looking."

"I think we should put our heads on all the gold coins from the crock of gold," said King Cormac. He too was in awe at the gold medallion with his image engraved into it. He was around many gold pieces all his life, but never before had he been so impressed with a piece of gold like this one.

"You're all serious about your heads aren't you?" said Princess Tara. "What about my head? She held up her gold medallion for all to see. "Isn't that gorgeous?"Doesn't that deserve to be heads up on all the gold coins everywhere?"

"Saints preserve us," said King Brian. "I know why there are no leprechaun Kings heads on any Irish coins? And no leprechaun Princess's heads on coins." He looked directly into Princess Tara's eyes.

"Why?" asked King Brendan, still staring at his head on the medallion.

"Because," said King Brian, "your heads would grow so big they would disappear off the coin and leave nothing but a freckle on them."

"I apologize for us getting carried away, Brian," smiled King Cormac. "We're just mesmerized with our own beauty on these medallions.

"Thank you so much Santa," said King Rory. "They truly are keepsakes, and we will treasure them forever."

The Rescueteers held their gold medallions close to their hearts and thanked Santa. Christmas prevails because of them. All were humbled and honored to receive this special gift with such powerful words from such a special person, Santa Claus.

"I must leave you all now," smiled Santa. "It's going to be a big night tonight." Santa turned to Rudolph and once again Rudolph did him the honors of kneeling on the ground for Santa to get on his back. Santa picked up his reins again and yelled the words, "Onward Rudolph, Up, Up, and away, ho, ho, ho."

In a moment, Santa and Rudolph were airborne and the red glow left Magandy's Pond. Rudolph cantered on back to the North Pole. The sound of his Christmas bells faded in the distance and the light from his nose disappeared into the night sky.

"Jeepers, said Nanny, "I forgot about the daylight."

"Let me wish it back, Nanny," said Ned. "I haven't wished for ages."

"Okay Ned," said Nanny as she stood back and gave Ned room to wish back the daylight.

Ned took a deep breath, he stood up straight and tall and said,

> "Last night is gone,
> I'm happy to say.
> Christmas Eve morning
> Is here today.
> May the sun rise
> Above our head,
> And may we all
> Go back to bed."

"Good job Ned Franey," said King Brian. "And what a good idea to go back to bed." He stretched his arms above his head and yawned. Then everybody yawned and stretched. Suddenly the night of high drama caught up with them and they felt exhausted. The sun peeped over the green hills of Coolrainy. The Rescueteers stood silhouetted side by side and in silence watched the sun rise. They quietly reflected on the night that was now behind them and they were thankful for the day ahead of them.

As the sun got brighter and rose higher they began to fade away. Nanny could feel the comfort of her bed and the warmth of her blankets. Henry Daly was snuggled in beside her with his head on her shoulder. In her sleepy daze, Nanny opened her hand and saw her gold medallion with her cowgirl profile engraved into it. She closed her hand and smiled. It really did happen.

"Shucks, Henry Daly," whispered Nanny, "we saved Santa Claus last night, now ain't that somethin'?"

"It sure is, Nanny Reilly," answered Henry in a scratchy whisper, "it sure is."

THE END

GLOSSARY

Aran sweater: An Irish knit sweater with various patterns.

Banshee: A witch of Irish folklore.

Boudoir: A lady's bedroom.

Departures: Where the victims of the Banshee are taken to become skeletees.

Leprechaun: A mischievous little person of Irish folklore.

Long in the tooth: An Irish expression for being wise.

Satchel: A small bag.

Shenanigans: Mischievous doings.

Skelechef: A skeleton chef in the Banshee's Cradle.

Skelecook: A skeleton cook in the Banshee's Cradle.

Skelechair: A chair made from bones.

Skelechaun: A skeleton leprechaun in the Banshee's Cradle.

Skeliform: A skeletee's uniform.

Skelengineer: A skeleton engineer in the Banshee's Cradle.

Skeleguard: A skeleton security guard in the Banshee's Cradle.

Skelelist: The Banshee's list of skeletees.

SkelOrientation Express: Victims of the Banshee arrive in the Banshee's Cradle on this train and go through orientation at skeleresources.

Skelassistant: A personal skeleton assistant to the Banshee.

Skelesource: A skeleton who works in the skeleresources department.

Skeleresources: Where all the victims of the Banshee are processed, given uniforms and sent to the necessary department.

Skeletee: An skeleton employee of the Banshee.

Skelattendants: A skeleton attendant.

Skeletrustee: A victim of the Banshee used to do temporary work before going through departures

Shillelagh: A blackthorn stick from the blackthorn tree of various sizes. Normally used as a walking stick. The Rescueteers use them as magic wands.

Tin whistle: An Irish flute.

Walls of Limerick: A traditional Irish dance, normally danced two opposite two.